D1492004

The
Pilgrim's Progress

AS JOHN BUNYAN WROTE IT:

BEING A FAC-SIMILE REPRODUCTION
OF THE
First Edition
PUBLISHED IN 1678

WITH AN INTRODUCTION
BY
DR. JOHN BROWN
AUTHOR OF 'JOHN BUNYAN AND HIS TIMES'

LONDON
ELLIOT STOCK, 62, PATERNOSTER ROW
1895

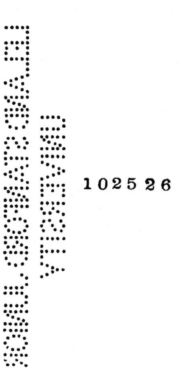

Preface.

___

... work here presented to the public
... an exact reproduction of the first
... of the first part of "The Pilgrim's
... Till recent years this book of
... fame was supposed to have been
... during Bunyan's twelve years' im-
... in Bedford Gaol. But as that
... terminated in the early part
... and the title of the first edition
... that the book was "Printed for
... Ponder at the Peacock in the
... near Cornhil, 1678," the ques-
... as to why there was this long
... between the writing of the work
... publication. Bunyan's own ac-
... the matter certainly does not seem
... any such delay. The early critics
... the book was submitted were, it
... divided as to whether it
... be or die:

... John, print it; others said, Not so;
... it might do good; others said, No."

... nothing for it but that the
... settle the matter for himself,
... to have done while the con-
troversy

inanity among these local critics was
going forward :

" At last I thought, Since you are thus divided,
I print it will; and so the case decided."

One feels in reading these lines that there
is a briskness in Bunyan's own account of
the matter not at all suggestive of a six
years' delay before sending the manuscript
to the printer. Yet there can be no doubt
that the book was written in gaol, for
when the third, which was the first com-
plete, edition of the work appeared in 1679,
Bunyan himself explained the meaning of
the word " den" in the text on the first
page by placing the words " the Jail" in the
margin. We have the best authority, there-
fore, for saying that the book was written
in prison, but then the question recurs,
during what imprisonment ? One of Bun-
yan's own contemporaries had told us that
he suffered a six months' imprisonment as
well as that which lasted for twelve years ;
we had been told also that Bishop Barlow,
as bishop of the diocese, had something to do
with Bunyan's release ; but Barlow was
not made Bishop of Lincoln till the summer
of 1675, and, therefore, could have had
nothing to do with the release of 1672.

Taking all the circumstances of the case
into account, the present writer ventured in
1885 to put forth the theory that after the
King tore off the Great Seal from the
Declaration of Indulgence, and the
preachers' licenses were recalled by pro-
clamation, Bunyan, who had then been
three years the pastor of the Bedford
Church,

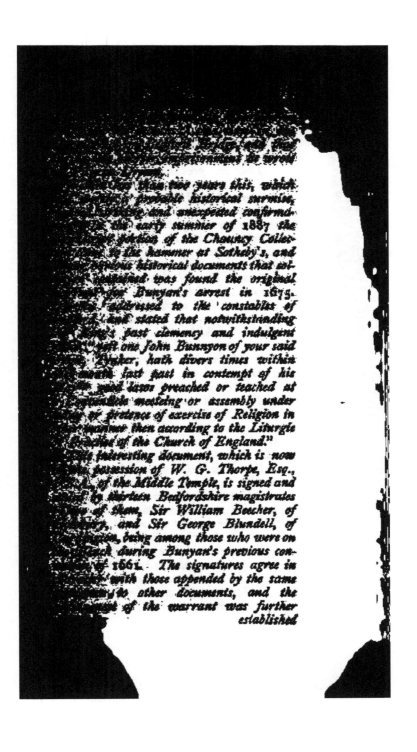

...than two years this, which ...probable historical surmise, ...y, and unexpected confirma- ...the early summer of 1887 the ...portion of the Chauncy Collec- ...to the hammer at Sotheby's, and ...ous historical documents that col- ...signed, was found the original ...for Bunyan's arrest in 1675. ...addressed to the constables of ...and stated that notwithstanding ...'s past clemency and indulgent ...one John Bunnyon of your said ...Tinker, hath divers times within ...last past in contempt of his ...good laws preached or teached at ...unlawful meeting or assembly under ...or pretence of exercise of Religion in ...manner then according to the Liturgie ...of the Church of England."

...interesting document, which is now ...possession of W. G. Thorpe, Esq., ...of the Middle Temple, is signed and ...by thirteen Bedfordshire magistrates ...them, Sir William Beecher, of ...and Sir George Blundell, of ...being among those who were on ...during Bunyan's previous con- ...1661. The signatures agree in ...with those appended by the same ...to other documents, and the ...of the warrant was further
established

Thus the probability almost amounts to
certainty that Bunyan was again in gaol
in 1675-76, and that during this second imprisonment of six months he wrote the
greater portion of the first part of the book
which has made his name immortal. We
say the greater portion, for, as the reader
will see, on turning to page 161 of this
facsimile, there is a curious break in the
narrative which seems to suggest that the
work was laid aside for a time and then
taken up again. After describing the
parting which took place between the
shepherds and the pilgrims on the Delectable Mountains, Bunyan says : " So I
awoke from my Dream." In the next
sentence he goes on to say : " And I slept,
and dreamed again, and saw the same two
Pilgrims going down the mountains along
the highway towards the city." Does this
break in the narrative, which was in no
way demanded by the exigencies of the story,
indicate that what went before was written
in the " certain place where was a den,"
and that what follows after was written in
his own home after the author's release?
It may be so ; at all events, it was still
some months after this second imprisonment
of his was over before the MS., about which
some of his neighbours had their misgivings,
found its way to the printer.

When ready for the larger world outside,
the book was entered in the Register of the
Stationers'

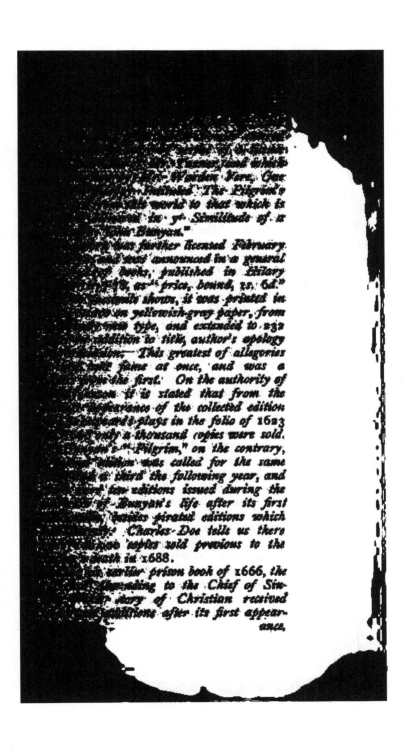

... ... which
... Worden Vere, Gue
... Intituled The Pilgrim's
... this worke to that which is
... to ye Similitude of a
... Bunyan."

... was further licensed February,
... and was announced in a general
... of books, published in Hilary
... es price, bound, 1s. 6d."
... shown, it was printed in
... on yellowish-gray paper, from
... type, and extended to 232
... addition to title, author's apology
... This greatest of allegories
... fame at once, and was a
... the first. On the authority of
... it is stated that from the
... appearance of the collected edition
... plays in the folio of 1623
... a thousand copies were sold.
... "Pilgrim," on the contrary,
... was called for the same
... a third the following year, and
... ten editions issued during the
... Bunyan's life after its first
... besides pirated editions which
... Charles Doe tells us there
... copies sold previous to the
... in 1688.

... earlier prison book of 1666, the
... to the Chief of Sin-
... story of Christian received
... additions after its first appearance.

once. If the following pages of this fac-simile be examined, it will be seen that in the first edition of the "Pilgrim's Pro-gress" there was no description of Chris-tian breaking his mind to his wife and children; no appearance of Mr. Worldly-Wiseman; no second meeting with Evan-gelist; no account given by Christian to Good-will at the wicket-gate of his own turning aside. Christian's discourse with Charity at the Palace Beautiful was added afterwards, as were the four lines on his leaving the palace. The other additions were: the third appearance of Evangelist to the Pilgrims as they were nearing Vanity Fair; the further account of Mr. By-ends' rich relations, with the conversa-tion which took place between him and the Pilgrims; the sight of Lot's wife turned to a pillar of salt, with the talk it occasioned; the whole account of Diffidence, the wife of Giant Despair; and, finally, the description of the Pilgrims being met on the farther side of the river by the King's trumpeters in white and shining raiment. The most important addition made to the second edition of 1678 was the introduction of Mr. Worldly-Wiseman; and to the third the enlargement of the story of Mr. By-ends. It was to this third edition of 1679 there was first added an illustrative engraving in the shape of a portrait of the author by Robert White.

This first edition of the first part of the "Pilgrim's Progress" was, on the whole, much more roughly spelt than the first edition of the second part, published six

years

... W ... for example,
... Diptford, Pliable and
... die, dye, dy; raiment
... We have such forms as
... wounded grievously, travailers,
... for age, two wit for to wit, bin
... thorow for through, tro for trow,
... for brth, strodled for straddled,
... strook, bewayling, toull, forraign,
... astounded, sloath, melancholly,
... chaulketh, carkass, and villian.
... is nothing to remark upon in the
... of the final consonant in such
... as generall, untill, and the like, for
... the seventeenth-century custom;
... Bunyan also doubles it in such words
... donn, scarr, quagg, and wagg;
... what was even more unusual, he
... the medial in such words as hazzard,
... fullon, eccho, shaddow, widdow.
... making his entries in the Bedford
... book when he was pastor, he often
... the final "e," and in this first
... of his allegory also we find wholesom,
... bridg, and knowledg; while he
... letter to give the old plural form
... braines, decaies, alwaies, paines,
... and the like. We have also such
... colloquialisms and irregularities as: Catch't
... brast for burst, maiest, didest,
... for to go, I should a been, practick,
... toside, let's go over, like for likely,
... ransak't, mist for missed, such
... I, you was, we was, two miles'
... and things prophanes. The
second

second edition had fewer mis-spellings, but more printers' errors. Some very characteristic marginalia found in this edition were left out in subsequent issues. We have such racy comments as these : " A man may have company when he sets out for heaven, and yet go thither alone ;" " A Christian can sing alone when God doth give him the joy of his heart ;" " O brave Talkative !" " Christian snibbeth his fellow ;" " Hopeful swaggers ;" " Christian roundeth off Demas ;" " O good riddance !" " They are whip't and sent on their way."

Five copies only of the actual first edition have survived to our own day. When Southey edited a new edition for Messrs. Murray and Major in 1830, he said : " It is not known in what year the ' Pilgrim's Progress' was first published, no copy of the first edition having as yet been discovered ; the second is in the British Museum. It is ' with additions,' and its date is 1678. . . . The earliest with which Mr. Major has been able to supply me, either by means of his own diligent inquiries, or the kindness of his friends, is that ' eighth e-di-ti-on' so humorously introduced by Gay, and printed, not for Ni-cho-las Bod-ding-ton, but for Nathaniel Ponder, at the Peacock in the Poultrey. near the church, 1682." Of the five copies of the first edition now known to exist, the one which came first to light is that which belonged to the late R. S. Holford, Esq., of Park Lane, and Westonbirt House, Tetbury, Gloucestershire, which was purchased with the rest of Lord Vernon's library,

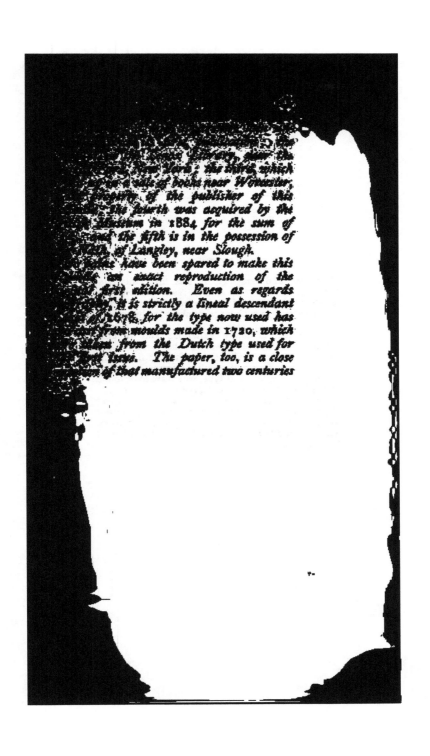

...Library, and the ... and one of the third, which ... a sale of books near Worcester, ... of the publisher of this ... the fourth was acquired by the ... Museum in 1884 for the sum of ... and the fifth is in the possession of ... of Langley, near Slough.

... have been spared to make this ... an exact reproduction of the ... first edition. Even as regards ... it is strictly a lineal descendant ... 1678, for the type now used has ... from moulds made in 1720, which ... from the Dutch type used for ... series. The paper, too, is a close ... of that manufactured two centuries

NOTE.

THE plan and language of this first edition of the *Pilgrim's Progress* are, in many places, very different from those of the modern editions, which are circulated in such large numbers in the present day.

There are so many variations and peculiar features in it, that those who have never seen the original form will be surprised at the many quaint expressions and peculiar phrases, as well as the curious spelling and type, which are to be found in the book as Bunyan first gave it to the world.

Believing that many admirers of the great allegory would be interested in seeing its earliest form, the publisher has issued the present edition, which faithfully reproduces all the peculiarities of the original.

THE
Pilgrim's Progress
FROM
THIS WORLD,
TO
That which is to come:

Delivered under the Similitude of a

DREAM

Wherein is Difcovered,
The manner of his fetting out,
His Dangerous Journey; And fafe
Arrival at the Defired Countrey.

I have ufed Similitudes, Hof. 12. 10.

By *John Bunyan.*

Licenfed and Entred according to Order.

LONDON,
Printed for *Nath. Ponder* at the *Peacock*
in the *Poultrey* near *Cornhil,* 1678.

THE
AUTHOR'S Apology
For his BOOK.

Hen at the firſt I took my Pen in hand,
　　Thus for to write ; I did not underſtand
That I at all ſhould make a little Book
In ſuch a mode ; Nay, I had undertook
To make another, which when almoſt done ;
Before I was aware, I this begun.

　And thus it was : I writing of the Way
And Race of Saints, in this our Goſpel-Day,
Fell ſuddenly into an Allegory
About their Journey, and the way to Glory,
In more than twenty things, which I ſet down ;
This done, I twenty more had in my Crown,
And they again began to multiply,
Like ſparks that from the coals of fire do fly.
Nay then, thought I, if that you breed ſo faſt,
I'll put you by your ſelves, leſt you at laſt
Should prove ad infinitum, and eat out
The Book that I already am about.

　Well, ſo I did ; but yet I did not think
To ſhew to all the World my Pen and Ink
In ſuch a mode ; I only thought to make
I knew not what : nor did I undertake
Thereby to pleaſe my Neighbour ; no not I ;
I did it mine own ſelf to gratifie.

　Neither did I but vacant ſeaſons ſpend
In this my Scribble ; nor did I intend

The Authors Apology for his Book.

But to divert my self in doing this,
From worser thoughts, which make me do amiss.

Thus I set Pen to Paper with delight,
And quickly had my thoughts in black and white.
For having now my Method by the end,
Still as I pull'd, it came ; and so I penn'd
It down, until it came at last to be
For length and breadth the bigness which you see.

Well, when I had thus put mine ends together,
I shew'd them others, that I might see whether
They would condemn them, or them justifie :
And some said, let them live ; some, let them die.
Some said, John, *print it ; others said, Not so :*
Some said, It might do good ; others said, No.

Now was I in a straight, and did not see
Which was the best thing to be done by me :
At last I thought, Since you are thus divided,
I print it will ; and so the case decided.

For, thought I ; Some, I see, would have it done,
Though others in that Channel do not run ;
To prove then who advised for the best,
Thus I thought fit to put it to the test.

I further thought, If now I did deny
Those that would have it thus, to gratifie,
I did not know but hinder them I might
Of that which would to them be great delight.

For those that were not for its coming forth,
I said to them, Offend you I am loth ;
Yet since your Brethren pleased with it be,
Forbear to judge, till you do further see.

If

... out how to pick the better
... give them better pallate;
... them than Expostulate.
... write in such a stile as this?
... a method too, and yet not miss
... good, thy good? why may it not be done?
... Clouds bring Waters, when the bright bring
... dewbright, if they their Silver drops (name
... defend, the Earth, by yielding Crops,
... promise to both, and carpeth not at either,
... treasures up the Fruit they yield together:
... commixes both, that in her Fruit
... can distinguish this from that, they suit
... well, when hungry: but if she be full,
... shuts out both, and makes their blessings null.
... see the ways the Fisher-man doth take
... catch the Fish; what Engins doth he make?
... how he ingageth all his Wits,
... his Snares, Lines, Angles, Hooks and Nets.
... Fish there be, that neither Hook, nor Line,
... Snare, nor Net, nor Engin can make thine;
... must be grop't for, and be tickled too,
... they will not be catcht, what e're you do.
... doth the Fowler seek to catch his Game,
... divers means, all which one cannot name?
... Gun, his Nets, his Lime-twigs, light, and bell;
... creeps, he goes, he stands; yea who can tell
... his Gestures, Yet there's none of these
... him master of what Fowls he please.

A 4   Yea,

Yea, he must Pipe, and Whistle to catch this;
Yet if he does so, that Bird he will miss.

   If that a Pearl may in a Toads-head dwell,
And may be found too in an Oister-shell;
If things that promise nothing, do contain
What better is then Gold; who will disdain,
(That have an inkling of it,) there to look,
That they may find it.   *Now my little Book,*
(Tho void of all those paintings that may make
It with this or the other Man to take,)
Is not without those things that do excel
What do in brave, but empty notions dwell.

   Well, yet I am not fully satisfied,
That this your Book will stand; when soundly try'd
   Why, what's the matter! it is dark, what tho?
But it is feigned. What of that I tro?
Some men by feigning words as dark as mine,
Make truth to spangle, and its rayes to shine.

   But they want solidness: Speak man thy mind,
They drown'd the weak; Metaphors make us blind.
   Solidity, indeed becomes the Pen
Of him that writeth things Divine to men:
But must I needs want solidness, because
By Metaphors I speak; Was not Gods Laws,
His Gospel-Laws, in oldertime held forth
By Types, Shadows and Metaphors? Yet loth
Will any sober man be to find fault
With them, lest he be found for to assault
The highest Wisdom.   *No, he rather stoops,*
And seeks to find out what by pins and loops,

... . And happy is he
... light, and grace that in them be:
... forward therefore to conclude,
... solidness, that I am rude:
... solid in shew, not solid be;
... in parables despise not we,
... most hurtful lightly we receive,
... that good are, of our souls bereave.
... dark and cloudy words they do but hold
... Truth, as Cabinets inclose the Gold.
The Prophets us'd much by Metaphors
... forth Truth; Yea, who so considers
... his Apostles too, shall plainly see,
... Truths to this day in such Mantles be.
... am I afraid to say that holy Writ,   [Wis,
... for its Stile, and Phrase puts down all
... where so full of all those things,
... Figures, Allegories,) yet there springs
... that same Book that lustre, and those rayes
... light, that turns our darkest nights to days.
... let my Carper, to his Life now look,
... said, There darker lines then in my Book
... any.   Yea, and let him know,
... his best things there are worse lines too.
... but stand before impartial men,
... One, I durst adventure Ten,
... will take my meaning in these lines
... them his Lies in Silver Shrines.

                                                Come,

Come, Truth, although in Swadling-clouts, I find
Informs the Judgement, rectifies the Mind,
Pleases the Understanding, makes the Will
Submit; the Memory too it doth fill
With what doth our Imagination please;
Likewise, it tends our troubles to appease.

    Sound words I know Timothy *is to use;*
And old Wives Fables he is to refuse,
But yet grave Paul, *him no where doth forbid*
The use of Parables; in which lay hid   (were
That Gold, those Pearls, and precious stones that
Worth digging for; and that with greatest care.

    Let me add one word more, O man of God!
Art thou offended? dost thou wish I had
Put forth my matter in an other dress,
Or that I had in things been more express?
Three things let me propound, then I submit
To those that are my betters, (as is fit.)
    1. *I find not that I am denied the use*
Of this my method, so I no abuse
Put on the Words, Things, Readers, or be rude
In handling Figure, or Similitude,
In application; but, all that I may,
Seek the advance of Truth, this or that way:
Denyed, did I say? Nay, I have leave,
(Example too, and that from them that have
God better pleased by their words or ways,
Then any man that breatheth now adays,)
Thus to express my mind, thus to declare
Things unto thee, that excellentest are.

                              2. *I*

... of their Fish there taken —
... Indeed if they abuse
... themselves, and, the craft they use
... intent; But yet let Truth be free
... her Salleys upon Thee, and Me,
... way it pleases God. For who knows how,
... then he that taught us first to Plow,
... our Mind and Pens for his Design?
... he makes base things usher in Divine.
... I find that holy Writ in many places (cases
... semblance with this method, where the
... call for one thing, to set forth another:
... it I may then, and yet nothing smother
Truths golden Beams; Nay, by this method may
... it cast forth its rayes as light as day.

... now, before I do put up my Pen,
... shew the profit of my Book, and then
... commit both thee, and it unto that hand (stand.
That pulls the strong down, and makes weak ones
... This Book it chaulketh out before thine eyes
The man that seeks the everlasting Prize:
... shews you whence he comes, whither he goes,
... What he leaves undone; also what he does:
... also shews you how he runs, and runs
Till he unto the Gate of Glory comes.

... shews too, who sets out for life amain,
... if the lasting Crown they would attain:
Here also you may see the reason why
... lose their labour, and like Fools do die.

This

The Authors Apology for his Book.

This Book will make a Travailer of thee,
If by its Counsel thou wilt ruled be;
It will direct thee to the Holy Land,
If thou wilt its Directions understand:
Yea, it will make the sloathful, active be;
The Blind also, delightful things to see.

Art thou for something rare, and profitable?
Wouldest thou see a Truth within a Fable?
Art thou forgetful? wouldest thou remember
From New-years-day to the last of December?
Then read my fancies, they will stick like Burs,
And may be to the Helpless, Comforters.

This Book is writ in such a Dialect,
As may the minds of listless men affect:
It seems a Novelty, and yet contains
Nothing but sound, and honest Gospel-strains.

Would'st thou divert thy self from Melancholly?
Would'st thou be pleasant, yet be far from folly?
Would'st thou read Riddles, & their Explanation?
Or else be drownded in thy Contemplation?
Dost thou love picking meat? or would'st thou see
A man i'th Clouds, and hear him speak to thee?
Would'st thou be in a Dream, and yet not sleep?
Or would'st thou in a moment laugh, and weep?
Wouldest thou loose thy self, and catch no harm?
And find thy self again without a charm? (what
Would'st read thy self, and read thou know'st not
And yet know whether thou art blest or not,
By reading the same lines? O then come hither,
And lay my Book, thy Head, and Heart together.

JOHN BUNYAN.

THE
Pilgrims Progress:

In the similitude of a

DREAM.

S I walk'd through the wildernefs of this world, I lighted on a certain place, where was a Denn; And I laid me down in that place to fleep: And as I flept I dreamed a Dream. I dreamed, and behold *I faw a Man* cloathed with Raggs, ftanding in a certain place, with his face from his own Houfe, a Book in his hand, and a great burden upon his back.* I looked, and faw him open the Book, and Read therein; and as he Read, he wept and trembled: and not being able longer to

contain,

*Ifa. 64. 6.
Lu. 14. 33.
Pf. 38. 4.
Hab. 2. 2
Act 16. 31.

contain, he brake out with a lamentable cry; saying, *what shall I do?*

I saw also that he looked this way, and that way, as if he would run; yet he stood still, because as I perceived, he could not tell which way to go. I looked then, and saw a Man named *Evangelist* coming to him, and asked, *Wherefore dost thou cry?* He answered, Sir, I perceive, by the Book in my hand, that I am Condemned to die, and *after that to come to Judgement; and I find that I am not *willing to do the first, nor *able to do the second.

Then said *Evangelist*, Why not willing to die? since this life is attended with so many evils? The Man answered, Because I fear that this burden that is upon my back, will finck me lower then the Grave; and I shall fall into *Tophet.* And Sir, if I be not fit to go to Prison, I am not fit (I am sure) to go to Judgement, and from thence to Execution; And the thoughts of these things make me cry.

Then said *Evangelist*, If this be thy condition, why standest thou still? He answered, Because I know not whither

*Heb. 9.
27.
*Job 16.
17, 22.
*Ezek.
36. 24.

*Isa. 30.
33.

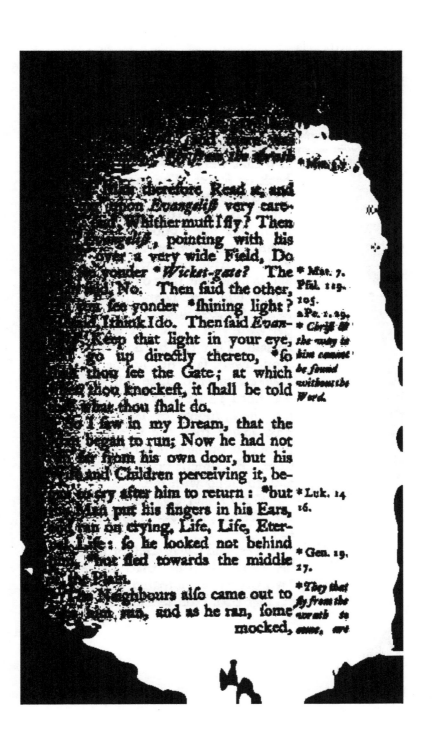

... therefore Read it, and
... upon *Evangelist* very care-
... Whither must I fly? Then
Evangelist, pointing with his
... over a very wide Field, Do
... yonder *Wicket-gate?* The   * Mat. 7.
... No. Then said the other,   Pfal. 119.
... fee yonder *shining light?   105.
... I think I do. Then said *Evan-*   a Pe. 1. 19.
... Keep that light in your eye,   the way to
... go up directly thereto, *fo   him cannot
... thou fee the Gate; at which   be found
... thou knockeft, it fhall be told   without the
... what thou fhalt do.   Word.
... I faw in my Dream, that the
... began to run; Now he had not
... from his own door, but his
... and Children perceiving it, be-
... cry after him to return : *but   * Luk. 14
... Man put his fingers in his Ears,   16.
... ran on crying, Life, Life, Eter-
... Life : fo he looked not behind
... but fled towards the middle   * Gen. 19.
... the Plain.   27.
... Neighbours alfo came out to   * They that
... him run, and as he ran, fome   fly from the
... mocked,   wrath to

A Coming stock in the world. Iſ. 20, 10

mocked, others threatned; and ſome cried after him to return: Now among thoſe that did ſo, there were two that were reſolved to fetch him back by force: The name of the one was *Obſtinate*, and the name of the other *Pliable*. Now by this time the Man was got a good diſtance from them; But however they were reſolved to purſue him; which they did, and in little time they over-took him. Then ſaid the Man, Neighbours, *Wherefore are you come?* They ſaid, To perſwade you to go back with us; but he ſaid, That can by no means be: You dwell, ſaid he, in the City of *Deſtruction* (the place alſo where I was born,) I ſee it to be ſo; and dying there, ſooner or later, you will ſink lower then the Grave, into a place that burns with Fire and Brimſtone; Be content good Neighbours, and go along with me.

* Obſtinate.

*What! ſaid Obſtinate, and leave our Friends, and our comforts behind us!

* Chriſtian.

* 2 Cor. 4. 18,

* Yes, ſaid *Chriſtian*, (for that was his name) becauſe that all is not *worthy to be compared with a little of that that I am ſeeking to enjoy,

and

... may ... ... for there
... ... enough, and to spare; ... Luk. 35.
... and prove my words.

*Obst. But are the things you seek,
since you leave all the World to find them?*

Chr. I seek an * *Inheritance, in-* * 1 Pet. 1. 4.
corruptible, undefiled, and that fadeth
away; and it is laid up in Heaven,
safe there, to be bestowed at the * Heb. 11.
... appointed, on them that dili- 16.
... seek it.

Obst. Tush, said *Obstinate, away with*
your Book; will you go back with us, or

Chr. No, not I, said the other; be-
cause I have laid my hand to the
... ... *Plow.* *Luk. 9. 62.

Obst. Come then, Neighbour Pliable,
let us turn again, and go home with-
out him; There is a Company of these
crasie-headed Coxcombs, that when
they take a fancy by the end, are wiser
in their own eyes then seven men that
can render a Reason.

Pli. Then said *Pliable,* Don't re-
vile; if what the good *Christian* says
is true, the things he looks after, are
better then ours : my heart inclines
... with my Neighbour.

Obst.

Obft. What! more Fools ftill? be ruled by me and go back; who knows whither fuch a brain-fick fellow will lead you? Go back, go back, and be wife.

Ch. Come with me Neighbour *Pliable*; there are fuch things to be had which I fpoke of, and many more Glories befides. If you believe not me, read here in this Book; and for the truth of what is expreft there-in, behold all is confirmed by the † blood of him that made it.

† Heb. 13.
10. 21,

Pli. Well Neighbour Obftinate *(faid* Pliable) *I begin to come to a point; I intend to go along with this good man, and to caft in my lot with him: But my good Companion, do you know the way to this defired place?*

Ch. I am directed by a man whofe name is *Evangelift*, to fpeed me to a little Gate that is before us, where we fhall receive inftruction about the way.

Pli. Come then good Neighbour, let us be going.

Then they went both together.

Obft. And I will go back to my place, faid *Obftinate*. I will be no Companion of fuch mifs-led fantafti-cal Fellows. Now

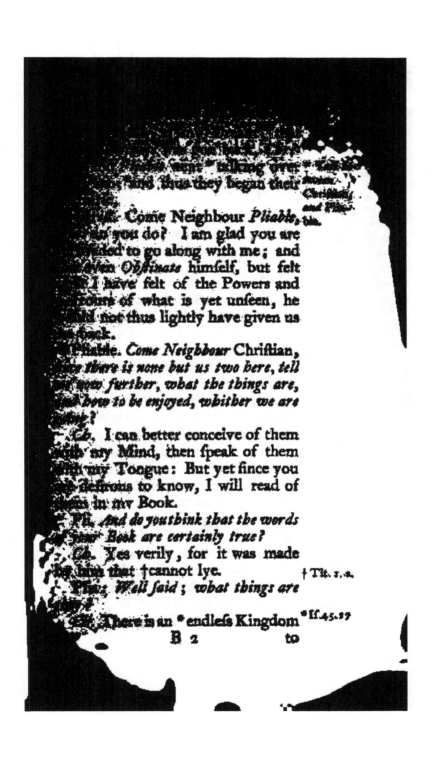

... went talking over ... <invisible>*</invisible> *now
... and thus they began their* <invisible>Christian</invisible> *discourse.* <invisible>Christian and Pli-able.</invisible>

... Come Neighbour *Pliable*,
... you do? I am glad you are
... to go along with me; and
... *Obstinate* himself, but felt
... I have felt of the Powers and
... of what is yet unseen, he
... not thus lightly have given us
... back.

Pliable. Come Neighbour Christian,
*... there is none but us two here, tell
... now further, what the things are,
... how to be enjoyed, whither we are
...?*

Ch. I can better conceive of them
... my Mind, then speak of them
... my Tongue: But yet since you
... desirous to know, I will read of
... in my Book.

*Pli. And do you think that the words
... Book are certainly true?*

Ch. Yes verily, for it was made
... him that †cannot lye.   † Tit. 1. 2.

*Pli. Well said; what things are
...?*

Ch. There is an *endless Kingdom *If. 45. 17

B 2   to

John 10. to be Inhabited, and everlasting life
17, 18, 29. to be given us; that we may Inhabit
that Kingdom for ever.

Pli. *Well said; and what else?*

Chr. There are Crowns of Glory
† 2 Tim. 4. to be given us; †and Garments that
8. will make us shine like the Sun in the
Rev. 3. 4. Firmament of Heaven.
Matth. 13.

Plia. *This is excellent; And what else?*

Cb. There shall be no more crying,
* Isa. 25.8. * nor sorrow; For he that is owner
Rev. 7. 16. of the places, will wipe all tears
17. from our eyes.
Cap. 21.4.

Pli. *And what company shall we have there?*

Cb. There we shall be with *Sera-*
* Isa 6. 2. *phims,* *and *Cherubins,* Creatures that
1 Thiss. 4. will dazle your eyes to look on them:
16. 17. There also you shall meet with thou-
Rev. 7. 17. sands, and ten thousands that have
gone before us to that place; none
of them are hurtful, but loving, and
holy: every one walking in the sight
of God; and standing in his presence
with acceptance for ever: In a
† Rev. 4. 4. word, there we shall see the † Elders
with their Golden Crowns: There
* Cha. 14. we shall see the Holy * Virgins with
1, 2, 3, 4, 5. their Golden Harps. There we
shall

... in the World ... burned in flames, ... Beasts, drowned in the ... the love that they bare to ... Lord of the place; all well, and ... with b Immortality, as with Garments.

b 2 Cor. 5. 2, 3, 5.

Pli. The hearing of this is enough to ... ones heart; but are these things ... enjoyed? how shall we get to be ... hereof?

Chr. The Lord, the Governour of ... Countrey, hath Recorded *that* ... this Book: The substance of ... is, if we be truly willing to ... it, he will bestow it upon us ...

c Isa. 55. 1, 2. Joh. 7. 37. Chap. 6. 37 Rev. 21. 6 Cap. 22. 17

Pli. Well, my good Companion, glad ... I to hear of these things: Come on, ... us mend our pace.

Chr. I cannot go so fast as I would, ... reason of this burden that is upon ... back.

Now I saw in my Dream, that just ... they had ended this talk, they ... near to a very *Miry Slough*, that ... in the midst of the Plain, and ... being heedless, did both fall ... into the bogg. The name ... was *Dispond*. Here therefore they wallowed for a time, being grievioufly bedaubed with the dirt; And *Chriftian*, becaufe of the burden that was on his back, began to fink in the Mire.

Pli. Then faid Pliable, *Ah, Neighbour* Chriftian, *where are you now?*

Ch. Truly, faid *Chriftian*, I do not know.

Pli. At that, *Pliable* began to be offended; and angerly faid to his Fellow, *Is this the happinefs you have told me all this while of? if we have fuch ill fpeed at our firft fetting out, what may we expeid, 'twixt this, and our Journeys end?* d *May I get out again with my life, you fhall poffefs the brave Country alone for me.* And with that he gave a defperate ftruggle or two, and got out of the Mire, on that fide of the Slough which was next to his own Houfe: So away he went, and *Chriftian* faw him no more.

Wherefore *Chriftian* was left to tumble in the Slough of *Difpondency* alone, but ftill he endeavoured to ftruggle to that fide of the Slough, that was ftill further e from his own Houfe, and next to the Wicket-gate; the which he did, but could not get out, becaufe

d *It is not enough to be Pliable.*

e *Chriftian in trouble, feeks ftill to get further from his own Houfe.*

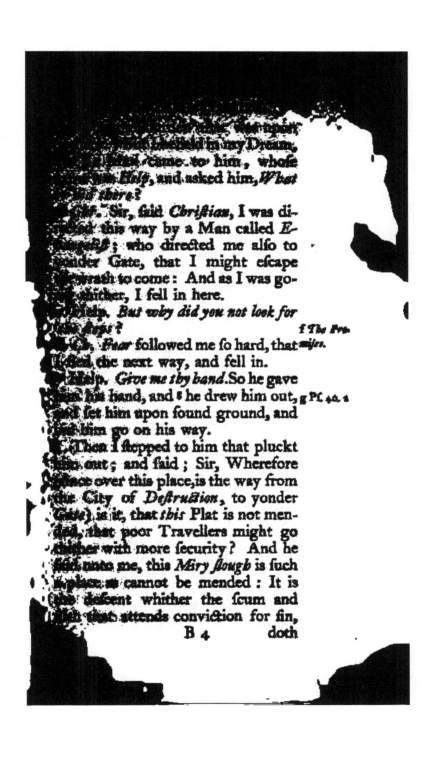

... beheld in my Dream, ... came to him, whose ... Help, and asked him, *What* ... there?

Chr. Sir, said *Christian*, I was di... this way by a Man called *E*... ; who directed me also to ... Gate, that I might escape ... wrath to come: And as I was go... thither, I fell in here.

Help. *But why did you not look for* ... *steps?*

Chr. *Fear* followed me so hard, that ... the next way, and fell in.

Help. *Give me thy hand.* So he gave ... his hand, and [g] he drew him out, and set him upon found ground, and ... him go on his way.

Then I stepped to him that pluckt ... out; and said; Sir, Wherefore ... over this place, is the way from ... City of *Destruction*, to yonder ... is it, that *this* Plat is not men... that poor Travellers might go ... with more security? And he ... unto me, this *Miry slough* is such ... place as cannot be mended: It is ... descent whither the scum and ... attends conviction for sin,

f The Pro-
mises.

g Pf. 40. 2

B 4   doth

continually run, and therefore is it
called the *Slough of Difpond*: for ftill as
the finner is awakened about his loft
condition, there arifeth in his foul
many fears, and doubts, and dif-
couraging apprehenfions, which all
of them get together, and fettle in
this place: And this is the reafon of
the badnefs of this ground.

h Ifa. 35.
3, 4.

 It is not the *h* pleafure of the King,
that this place fhould remain fo bad;
his Labourers alfo, have by the direction of His Majefties Surveyors,
been for above this fixteen hundred
years, imploy'd about this patch of
ground, if perhaps it might have
been mended: yea, and to my knowledge, faith he, *Here* hath been fwal-
lowed up, at leaft Twenty thoufand Cart Loads; Yea Millions of
wholefom Inftructions, that have at
all feafons been brought from all
places of the Kings Dominions; (and
they that can tell, fay, they are
the beft Materials to make good
ground of the place;) If fo be it might
have been mended, but it is the *Slough
of Difpond* ftill; and fo will be, when
they have done what they can. •

 True, there are by the direction of
the

[illegible] certain good and substantial Steps, placed even through the very midst of this *Slough*; but at such time as this place doth much spue out its filth, as it doth against change of weather, these steps are hardly seen; or if they be, Men through the diziness of their heads, step besides; and then they are bemired to purpose, notwithstanding the steps be there; but the ground is good when they are once got in at the Gate.

The Promises of forgiveness and acceptance to life by faith in Christ.

k 1 Sa. 12. 23.

Now I saw in my Dream, that by this time *Pliable* was got home to his House again. So his Neighbours came to visit him; and some of them called him wise Man for coming back; and some called him Fool, for hazarding himself with *Christian*; others again did mock at his Cowardliness; saying, Surely since you began to venture, I would not have been so base to have given out for a few difficulties. So *Pliable* sat sneaking among them. But at last he got more confidence, and then they all turned their tales, and began to deride poor *Christian* behind his back. And thus much concerning *Pliable*.

By

By this time, *Chriſtian* was got up
to the Gate. Now over the Gate
there was Written, *Knock and it ſhall*
1 Matt.7.8. *be opened unto you.* [1] He knocked
therefore, more then once or twice,
ſaying,

May I now enter here? will he within
Open to ſorry me, though I have bin
An undeſerving Rebel? then ſhall I
Not fail to ſing his laſting praiſe on high.

At laſt there came a grave Perſon to
the Gate, named *Good-will*, who asked
Who was there? and whence he came?
and what he would have?

Ch. Here is a poor burdened ſinner,
I come from the City of *Deſtruction*,
but am going to Mount *Zion*, that I
may be delivered from the wrath to
come; I would therefore, Sir, ſince
I am informed that by this Gate is the
way thither, know if you are *willing*
to let me in.

m *The Gate*   *Good-will.* [m] I am *willing* with all
will be   my heart, ſaid he; and with that he
opened to opened the Gate.
broken-
hearted ſin-   So when *Chriſtian* was ſtepping in,
ners.   the other gave him a pull; Then ſaid
Chriſtian, what means that? The o-
ther

a lastey re-
vler thofe
that enter
the ſtraight
Gate.

... erected a ſtrong
... the Beelzebub is the
... from thence both he, and
... that are with him ſhoot Ar-
... thoſe that come up to this
... if happily they may dye be-
... they can enter in.   Then ſaid
... en, I rejoyce and tremble. So
... he was got in, the Man of the
... asked him, Who directed him
...

Ch. Evangeliſt bid me come hither
... knock, (as I did;) And he ſaid, that
... Sir, would tell me what I muſt
...

Good Will. An open Door is ſet be-
... thee, and no man can ſhut it.
Ch. Now I begin to reap the bene-
... of my hazzards.
Good Will. But how is it that you
... alone?
Ch. Becauſe none of my Neighbours ſaw their danger, as I ſaw mine.
Good Will. Did any of them know
of your coming?
Ch. Yea, my Wife and Children
... me at the firſt, and called after
... to turn again: Alſo ſome of my
Neigh-

Neighbours stood crying, and calling after me to return; but I put my Fingers in mine Ears, and so came on my way.

Good Will. *But did none of them follow you, to perswade you to go back?*

Ch. Yes, both *Obstinate*, and *Pliable*: But when they saw that they could not prevail, *Obstinate* went railing back; but *Pliable* came with me a little way.

Good Will. *But why did he not come through?*

Ch. We indeed came both together, until we came at the Slow of *Dispond*, into the which, we also suddenly fell. And then was my Neighbour *Pliable* discouraged, and would not adventure further.° Wherefore getting out again, on that side next to his own House; he told me, I should possess the brave Countrey alone for him: So he went his way, and I came mine. He after *Obstinate*, and I to this Gate.

° *A Man may have Company when he sets out for Heaven, & yet go thither alone.*

Good Will. Then said *Good Will*, Alas poor Man, is the Cœlestial Glory of so small esteem with him, that he counteth it not worth running the hazards of a few difficulties to obtain it. Well good *Christian*, come

a

... I will ...
... way thou must go:
... thee; dost thou see this
... way? That is the way thou
... go. It was cast up by the Patri-
... Prophets, Christ, his Apostles;
... it is as straight as a Rule can
... it. This is the way thou must go.
... But said *Christian*, *Is there no*
turnings nor windings by which a
stranger may loose the way?

Good Will. Yes, there are many
... *Bats* down upon this; and they
... Crooked, and Wide: But *thus*
thou may'st distinguish the right from
the wrong, *That* only being straight
and narrow.

Then I saw in my Dream, That
Christian asked him further, If he
could not help him off with his burden that was upon his back; For as
yet he had not got rid thereof, nor
could he by any means get it off
without help.

He told him; As to the burden, be
content to bear it, untill thou comest p *There is*
to the place of ᵖ Deliverance; for *no deliver-*
there it will fall from thy back it self. *rance from*
the guilt,
Then *Christian* began to gird up *and burden*
... *loins*, and to address himself to *of sin, but*
his

to sinners; even as also thou seest
ᵃ him stand as if he Pleaded with
Men: And whereas thou seest the
World as cast behind him, and that a
Crown hangs over his head; that is,
to shew thee that slighting and de-
spising the things that are present,
for the love that he hath to his Masters service, he is sure in the World
that comes next to have Glory for
his Reward: Now, said the *Interpreter*, I have shewed thee this Picture,
ᵇ *Why he
shewed him
the Picture
first.*
first, ᵇ because the Man whose Picture
this is, is the only Man, whom the
Lord of the Place whither thou art
going, hath Authorized, to be thy
Guide in all difficult places thou
mayest meet with in the way: wherefore take good heed to what I have
shewed thee, and bear well in thy
mind what thou hast seen; lest in thy
Journey, thou meet with some that
pretend to lead thee right, but their
way goes down to death.

Then he took him by the hand, and
led him into a very large *Parlour*
that was full of dust, because never
swept; the which, after he had re-
viewed a little while, the *Interpreter*
called for a man to *sweep*: Now
when

... to sweep the ... ... to fly about, that ... ... almoſt therewith been ... Then ſaid the *Interpreter* to ... that ſtood by, Bring hither ... and ſprinkle the Room; which ... ſhe had done, was ſwept and ... with pleaſure.

... Then ſaid Chriſtian, *What means* ...

... The *Interpreter* anſwered; ... Parlor is the heart of a Man ... was never ſanctified by the ſweet ... of the Goſpel: The *duſt*, is ... Original Sin, and inward Corrup- ... that have defiled the whole ... Man; He that began to ſweep at ... is the Law; but She that brought ... water, and did ſprinkle it, is the Go- ... Now, whereas thou ſaweſt that ... ſoon as the firſt began to ſweep, the ... duſt did ſo fly about that the ... Room by him could not be cleanſed, ... that thou waſt almoſt choaked ... therewith. This is to ſhew thee, that ... the Law, inſtead of cleanſing the ... heart (by its working) from ſin, d d Rom. 7. 6. ... doth revive, put e ſtrength into, and e 1 Cor. 15. ... increaſe it in the ſoul, as it doth 56. f Ro. 5. 20.

C　　　　　diſ-

discover and forbid it, but doth not give power to subdue.

Again, as thou sawest the *Damsel* sprinkle the Room with Water, upon which it was cleansed with pleasure: This is to shew thee, that when the Gospel comes in the sweet and precious influences thereof to the heart, then I say, even as thou sawest the Damsel lay the dust by sprinkling the Floor with Water, so is sin vanquished and subdued, and the soul made clean, through the Faith of it; and consequently g fit for the King of Glory to inhabit.

I saw moreover in my Dream, h that the *Interpreter* took him by the hand, and had him into a little Room; where sat two little Children, each one in his Chair: The name of the eldest was *Passion*, and of the other *Patience*; *Passion* seemed to be much discontent, but *Patience* was very quiet. Then *Christian* asked, What is the reason of the discontent of *Passion*? The *Interpreter* answered, The Governour of them would have him stay for his best things till the beginning of the next year; but he will have all now: i But *Patience* is willing to wait. Then

g Joh. 15. 3.
Eph. 5. 26.
Act. 15. 9.
Rom. 16.
25, 26.
Joh. 15.
13.

h *He shewed him Passion & Patience.*

Passion will have all now.

i *Patience is for waiting.*

...came to a Pil...
...him a Bag of Trea-...
...poured it down at his feet;...
...he took up, and rejoyced
...and withall, laughed Pa-
...to scorn: But I beheld but a
...and he had [1] lavished all a-
...and had nothing left him but

[1] And quickly lavishes all away.

Ch. Then said Christian to the Inter-
...ter, [m] Expound this matter more
...ly to me.

[m] The matter expounded.

In. So he said, These two Lads are
Figures; *Passion*, of the Men of *this*
World; and *Patience*, of the Men of
that which is to come: For as here
thou seest, *Passion will have all now*,
this year; that is to say, in *this* World;
So are the Men of this World: they
must have all their good things now,
they cannot stay till next *Year*; that
is, untill the *next* World, for their
Portion of good. That Proverb, *A
Bird in the Hand is worth two in the
Bush*, is of more Authority with
them, then are all the Divine Testi-
monies of the good of the World to
come. But as thou sawest, that he
had quickly lavished all away, and
had presently left him, nothing but

[n] The Worldly Man for a Bird in the hand.

C 2   Raggs;

Raggs; So will it be with all such Men at the end of this World.

Ch. Then said Christian, *Now I see* that Patience *has the best* a *Wisdom; and that upon many accounts.* 1. *Because he stays for the best things.* 2. *And also because he will have the Glory of His, when the other hath nothing but Raggs.*

a Patience
had the best
Wisdom.

In. Nay, you may add another; to wit, The glory of the *next* World will never wear out; but these are suddenly gone. Therefore *Passion* had not so much reason to laugh at *Patience,* because he had his good things first, as *Patience* will have to laugh at *Passion,* p because he had his best things *last;* for *first* must give place to *last,* because *last* must have his time to come, but *last* gives place to *nothing;* for there is not another to succeed: he therefore that hath his Portion *first,* must needs have a time to spend it; but he that has his Portion *last,* must have it lastingly. Therefore it is said of q *Dives, In thy lifetime thou hadest,* or *receivedest thy good things, and likewise* Lazarus *evil things; But now he is comforted, and thou art tormented.*

Things that
are first
must give
place, but
things that
are last, are
lasting.

q Luk. 16.
Dives had
his good
things first.

Ch.

... are not ...
... are now; but to wait
... to come.

... say the Truth; *For the things that are seen, are* Temporal; *but the things that are not seen, are* Eternal : *But though this be so; yet since things present,* and our fleshly appetite, *are such near Neighbours one to another ; and again,* because things to come, *and* carnal sense, are such strangers *one* to another : therefore it is, that *the first* of these so suddenly fall into *unity,* and that *distance* is so continued between the second.

Then I saw in my Dream, that the *Interpreter* took *Christian* by the hand, and led him into a place, where was a Fire burning against a Wall, and one standing by it always, casting much Water upon it to quench it. Yet did the Fire burn higher and hotter.

Then said Christian, *What means this?*

The *Interpreter* answered, This fire is the work of Grace that is wrought in the heart; he that casts Water upon it, to extinguish and put it out, is the *Devil:* but in that thou feeft the fire notwithstanding burn higher and hotter, thou shalt also see the reason of that: So he had him about to the back side of the Wall, where he saw a Man with a Veffel of Oyl in his hand, of the which he did also continually caft, but fecretly, into the fire. Then faid *Chriftian*, *What means this?* The *Interpreter* anfwered, This is *Chrift*, who continually with the Oyl of his Grace, maintains the work already begun in the heart; By the means of which, notwithftanding what the Devil can do, the souls of his People prove gracious ftill. And in that thou faweft, that the Man ftood behind the Wall to maintain the fire; this is to teach thee, that it is hard for the tempted to fee how this work of Grace is maintained in the foul.

2 Cor. 12. 9

I faw alfo that the *Interpreter* took him again by the hand, and led him into a pleafant place, where was builded a ftately Palace, beautiful to behold; at the fight of which, *Chriftian* was greatly delighted; he faw also upon the top thereof, certain Perfons walked, who were cloathed all in Gold. Then faid *Chriftian*, May

we

Then the Interpre-
ter took him, and led him up toward the door of the Palace; and
behold, at the door stood a great
Company of men, as desirous to go
in, but durst not.   There also sat a
Man, at a little distance from the
door, at a Table-side, with a Book,
and his Inkhorn before him, to take
the Name of him that should enter
therein: He saw also that in the door-
way, stood many Men in Armour to
keep it; being resolved to do to the
Man that would enter, what hurt and
mischief they could.   Now was *Chri-*
stian somwhat in a muse: at last, when
every Man started back for fear of the
Armed Men; *Christian* saw a Man of
a very stout countenance come up to
the Man that sat there to write; saying, Set down my name, Sir; the which
when he had done, he saw the Man
draw his Sword, and put an Helmet
upon his Head, and rush toward the
door upon the Armed Men, who laid
upon him with deadly force; but the
Man, not at all discouraged, fell to
cutting and hacking most fiercely; so,
after he had u received and given Act. 14, 22
many wounds to those that attempt-

C 4   ed

ted to keep him out, he cut his way
through them all, and preffed forward into the Palace ; at which there
was a pleafant voice heard from
thofe that were within, even of the
Three that walked upon the top of
the Palace.

Come in, Come in;
Eternal Glory thou fhalt win.

So he went in, and was cloathed with
fuch Garments as they. Then *Chri-*
ftian fmiled, and faid, I think verily I
know the meaning of this.

Now, faid *Chriftian*, let me go
hence : Nay ftay (faid the *Interpre-*
ter,) till I have fhewed thee a little
more, and after that thou fhalt go
on thy way. So he took him by the
hand again, and led him into a very
dark Room, where there fat a Man
in an Iron *Cage.

x *Defpair*
fits on Iron
Cage.

Now the Man, to look on, feem-
ed very fad: he fat with his eyes looking down to the ground, his hands
folded together ; and he fighed as if
he would break his heart. Then faid
Chriftian, What means this? At which
the *Interpreter* bid him talk with the
Man.

Chr. Then faid *Chriftian* to the
Man,

*. . . the Man an-
. . . . *I was not once.*
Chr. What wast thou once?

Man. The *Man* said, I was once
a fair and flourishing Profeſſor, both
in mine own eyes, and alſo in the
eyes of others: I once was, as I
thought, fair for the Cœleſtial City,
and had then even joy at the thoughts
that I ſhould get thither.

Chr. *Well, but what art thou now?*

Man. I am *now* a Man of Deſpair,
and am ſhut up in it, as in this Iron
Cage. I cannot get out; O *now* I
cannot.

Chr. *But how cameſt thou in this
condition?*

Man. I left off to watch, and be
ſober; I laid the reins upon the neck
of my luſts; I ſinned againſt the light
of the Word, and the goodneſs of
God: I have grieved the Spirit, and
he is gone; I tempted the Devil, and
he is come to me; I have provoked
God to anger, and he has left me; I
have ſo hardened my heart, that I
cannot repent.

Then ſaid *Chriſtian* to the *Interpreter,* But is there no hopes for ſuch a
Man as this? Ask him, ſaid the *In-*

terpreter? Nay, said *Christian*, pray Sir, do you.

Inter. Then said the *Interpreter, Is there no hope but you must be kept in this Iron Cage of Despair?*

Man. No, none at all.

Inter. *Why? the Son of the Blessed is very pitiful.*

Man. I have ⁷ Crucified him to my self, a fresh. I have despised ᶻ his Person, I have despised his Righteousness, I have counted his Blood an unholy thing, I have done despite ᵃ to the Spirit of Grace: Therefore I have shut my self out of all the Promises; and there now remains to me nothing but threatnings, dreadful threatnings, faithful threatnings of certain Judgement, which shall devour me as an Adversary.

Inter. *For what did you bring your self into this condition?*

Man. For the Lusts, Pleasures, and Profits of this World; in the injoyment of which, I did then promise my self much delight: but now even every one of those things also bite me, and gnaw me like a burning worm.

In-

y Heb. 6. 6.
z Luke 19. 14.

a Heb. 10. 28, 29.

tian. God hath denied me repentance; his Word gives me no encouragement to believe; yea, himself hath shut me up in this Iron Cage; nor can all the men in the World let me out. O Eternity! Eternity! how shall I grapple with the misery that I must meet with in Eternity!

Inter. Then said the *Interpreter* to *Christian*, Let this mans misery be remembered by thee, and be an everlasting caution to thee.

Chr. Well, said *Christian*, this is fearful; God help me to watch and be sober; and to pray, that I may shun the causes of this mans misery. Sir, is it not time for me to go on my way now?

Inter. Tarry till I shall shew thee one thing more, and then thou shalt go on thy way.

So he took *Christian* by the hand again, and led him into a Chamber, where there was one a rising out of Bed; and as he put on his Rayment, he shook and trembled. Then said *Christian*, Why doth this Man thus tremble? The *Interpreter* then bid

him

him tell to *Christian* the reafon of his
fo doing, So he began, and faid: This
night as I was in my fleep, I Dreamed,
and behold the Heavens grew exceeding black; alfo it thundred and
lightned in moft fearful wife, that it
put me into an Agony. So I looked
up in my Dream, and faw the Clouds
rack at an unufual rate; upon which
I heard a great found of a Trumpet,
and faw alfo a Man fit upon a Cloud,
attended with the thoufands of Heaven; they were all in flaming fire, alfo
the Heavens was on a burning flame.
I heard then a voice, faying, *Arife ye
Dead, and come to Judgement*; and
with that, the Rocks rent, the Graves
opened, & the Dead that were therein, came forth; fome of them were
exceeding glad, and looked upward;
and fome fought to hide themfelves
under the Mountains: Then I faw
the Man that fat upon the Cloud,
open the Book; and bid the World
draw near. Yet there was by reafon
of a Fiery flame that iffued out and
came from before him, a convenient
diftance betwixt him and them, as
betwixt the Judge and the Prifoners
at the Bar. I heard it alfo proclaimed

to

*2 Cor. 15.
1 Theff. 4.
Jude 15.
2 Thef.1.8.
Job. 5.28.
Rev. 20. 11
12, 13, 14.
If. 26. 21.
Mic. 7.16,
7.
Pf.5.1,2,3.
Dan.7.10.

Ch... Mal. 4. 1.

... tended in the Man...
...the Cloud; *Gather toge-*
...*the Tares, the Chaff, and Stubble,*
...cast them into the burning Lake;
...with that, the Bottomless pit o-
pened, just whereabout I stood; out
of the mouth of which there came in
an abundant manner Smoak, and
Coals of fire, with hideous noises. It
was also said to the same persons;
Gather my Wheat into my Garner.
And with that I saw many catch't up d 1 Thes.4.
16, 17.
and carried away into the Clouds,
but I was left behind. I also sought
to hide my self, but I could not; for
the Man that sat upon the Cloud, still
kept his eye upon me: my sins also Ro. 2. 14,
15.
came into mind, and my Conscience
did accuse me on every side. Upon
this I awaked from my sleep.

Chr. But what was it that made you
so fraid of this sight?

Man. Why I thought that the day
of Judgement was come, and that I
was not ready for it: but this frighted
me most, that the Angels gathered
up several, and left me behind; also
the pit of Hell opened her mouth
just where I stood: my Conscience too
within afflicted me; and as I thought,
the

the Judge had always his eye upon me, shewing indignation in his countenance.

Then said the *Interpreter* to *Christian*, Haſt thou conſidered all theſe things?

Chri. Yes, and they put me in *hope* and *fear.*

Inter. Well, keep all things ſo in thy mind, that they may be as a *Goad* in thy ſides, to prick thee forward in the way thou muſt go. Then *Christian* began to gird up his loins, and to addreſs himſelf to his Journey. Then ſaid the *Interpreter*, The Comforter be always with thee good *Christian*, to guide thee in the way that leads to the City.

So *Christian* went on his way, ſaying,

Here I have ſeen things rare, and pro-
    fitable;
Things pleaſant, dreadful, things to
    make me ſtable
In what I have began to take in hand:
Then let me think on them, and under-
    ſtand
Wherefore they ſhewed me was, and let
    me be
Thankful, O good Interpreter, to thee.

Now

I saw in my Dream, that the high way up which Christian was to go, was fenced on either side with a Wall, and that Wall is called Sal-vation. Up this way therefore did burdened Christian run, but not with-out great difficulty, because of the load on his back.

He ran thus till he came at a place somewhat ascending; and upon that place stood a Cross, and a little be-low in the bottom, a Sepulcher. So I saw in my Dream, that just as Christian came up with the Cross, his burden loosed from off his Shoulders, and fell from off his back; and be-gan to tumble, and so continued to do, till it came to the mouth of the Sepulcher, where it fell in, and I saw it no more.

Then was Christian glad e and lightsom, and said with a merry heart, *He hath given me rest, by his sorrow; and life, by his death.* Then he stood still a while, to look and wonder; for it was very surprizing to him, that the sight of the Cross should thus ease him of his burden. He looked therefore, and looked again, even till the springs that were in his head sent

e *When God re-leases us of our guilt and bur-den, weary as those that leap for joy.*

Zach. 12. 20. sent the 'waters down his cheeks. Now as he stood looking and weeping, behold three shining ones came to him, and saluted him, with *Peace be to thee*: so the first said to him, *Thy sins be forgiven.* The second, stript him of his Rags, and cloathed him with change of Raiment. The third also set a mark in his fore-head, and gave him a Roll with a Seal upon it, which he bid him look on as he ran, and that he should give it in at the Cœlestial Gate: so they went their way. Then *Christian* gave three leaps for joy, and went out singing,

A Christian can sing tho alone, when God doth give him the joy of his heart.

Thus far did I come loaden with my sin ;
Nor could ought ease the grief that I was in,
Till I came hither: What a place is this!
Must here be the beginning of my bliss!
Must here the burden fall from off my back?
Must here the strings that bound it to me, crack?
Blest Cross! blest Sepulcher! blest rather be
The Man that there was put to shame for me.

I

I saw in my Dream, that he went on thus, even untill he came to a bottom, where he saw, a little out of the way, three Men fast asleep with Fetters upon their heels. The name of the one was *Simple*, another *Sloth*, and the third *Presumption*.

a *Simple, Sloth,* and *Presumpti-on.*

Christian then seeing them lye in this case, went to them, if peradventure he might awake them. And cryed, You are like them that sleep on the top of a Mast, for the dead Sea is under you, a Gulf that hath no bottom: Awake therefore and come away, be willing also, and I will help you off with your Irons. He also told them, If he that goeth about like a roaring Lion comes by, you will certainly become a prey to his teeth. With that they lookt upon him, and began to reply in this sort: b *Simple* said, *I see no danger*; *Sloth* said, *Yet a little more sleep*: and *Presumption* said, *Every Fatt must stand upon his own bottom, what is the answer else that I should give thee?* And so they lay down to sleep again, and *Christian* went on his way.

b *There is no perswasion will do, if God openeth not the eyes.*

D   Yet

Yet was he troubled to think, That
men in that danger should so little
esteem the kindness of him that so
freely offered to help them; both by
awakening of them, counselling of
them, and proffering to help them off
with their Irons. And as he was
troubled there-about, he espied two
Men come tumbling over the Wall,
on the left hand of the narrow way;
and they made up a pace to him. The
name of the one was *Formalist*, and
the name of the other *Hypocrisie*. So,
as I said, they drew up unto him,
who thus entered with them into discourse.

Chr. *Gentlemen, Whence came you,
and whither do you go?*

Form. and *Hyp.* We were born in
the Land of Vain-glory, and are going for praise to Mount *Sion.*

Chr. *Why came you not in at the
Gate which standeth at the beginning
of the way? Know you not that it is
written.* Joh. 10. 1. *That he that cometh not in
by the door, but climbeth up some o-
ther way, the same is a thief and a
robber?*

Form. and *Hyp.* They said, That
to go to the Gate for entrance, was
by

... they then counted ... ... and that therefore ... way was to make a short ... of it, and to climb over as they ... done.

Chr. But will it not be counted a trespass, against the Lord of the City whither we are bound, thus to violate his revealed will?

Form. and *Hyp.* They told him, *"*That as for that, he needed not to trouble his head thereabout: for what they did, they had custom for; and could produce, if need were, Testimony that would witness it, for more then a thousand years.

Chr. *But,* said Christian, *Will your Practice stand a Trial at Law?*

Form. & *Hyp.* They told him, That Custom, it being of so long a standing, as above a thousand years, would doubtless now be admitted as a thing legal, by any Impartial Judge. And besides, said they, so be we get into the way, what's matter which way we get in; if we are in, we are in: thou art but in the way, who, as we perceive, came in at the Gate; and we are also in the way, that came

d *They that come into the way, but not by the door, think that they can say something in vindication of their own Practice.*

D 2   tum-

tumbling over the wall: Wherein now
is thy condition better then ours?

Chr. I walk by the Rule of my
Mafter, you walk by the rude working of your fancies. You are counted
thieves already, by the Lord of the
way; therefore I doubt you will
not be found true men at the end of
the way. You come in by your felves
without his direction, and fhall go
out by your felves without his mercy.

To this they made him but little
anfwer; only they bid him look to
himfelf. Then I faw that they went
on every man in his way, without
much conference one with another;
fave that thefe two men told *Chriftian*, That, as to *Laws and Ordinances*,
they doubted not but they fhould as
confcientioufly do them as he. Therefore faid they, We fee not wherein
thou differeft from us, but by the
Coat that is on thy back, which was,
as we tro, given thee by fome of thy
Neighbours, to hide the fhame of
tGal.2.16. thy nakednefs.

Chr. By ᵉ Laws and Ordinances,
you will not be faved, fince you came
not in by the door. And as for this
Coat that is on my back, it was given
me

...the Lord of the place whither
...and that, as you say, to cover
...nakedness with. And I take it as
...token of his kindness to me, for I
...had nothing but rags before. And
besides, thus I comfort my self as I
go: Surely, think I, when I come to
the Gate of the City, the Lord thereof will know me for good, since I
have his Coat on my back; a Coat
that he gave me freely in the day that
he stript me of my rags. I have moreover a mark in my forehead, of
which perhaps you have taken no
notice, which one of my Lords most
intimate Associates, fixed there in the
day that my burden fell off my
shoulders. I will tell you moreover,
that I had then given me a Roll sealed
to comfort me by reading, as I go in
the way; I was also bid to give it in
at the Coelestial Gate, in token of
my certain going in after it: all
which things I doubt you want, and
want them, because you came not
in at the Gate.

To these things they gave him no
answer, only they looked upon each
other and *laughed*. Then I saw that
they went on all, save that *Christian*

*f Christian
has got his
Lords Coat
on his back,
and is com-
forted
therewith,
he is com-
forted also
with his
Mark, and
his Roll.*

kept before, who had no more talk but with himfelf, and that fomtimes fighingly, and fomtimes comfortably: alfo he would be often reading in the Roll that one of the fhining ones gave him, by which he was refrefhed.

I beheld then, that they all went on till they came to the foot of an Hill, ^g at the bottom of which was a Spring. There was alfo in the fame place two other ways befides that which came ftraight from the Gate; one turned to the left hand, and the other to the right, at the bottom of the Hill: but the narrow way lay right up the Hill (and the name of the going up the fide of the Hill, is called *Difficulty*.) *Chriftian* now went to the Spring and drank thereof to refrefh himfelf, and then began to go up the Hill; faying,

g He comes to the hill Difficulty.

This Hill though high, I covet to afcend;
The difficulty will not me offend;
For I perceive the way to life lies here;
Come, pluck up, Heart; lets neither faint
   nor fear :
Better, tho difficult, th'right way to go,
Then wrong, though eafie, where the end
   is wo.

The

... these two also came to the foot of the Hill: But when they saw that the Hill was steep and high, and that there was two other ways to go ; and suppofing alfo, that thefe two ways might meet again, with that up which *Chriftian* went, on the other fide of the Hill : Therefore they were re- folved to go in thofe ways (now the name of one of thofe ways was *Danger*, and the name of the other *Deftruction*.) So [h] the one took the way which is called *Danger*, which led him into a great Wood ; and the other took directly up the way to De- *ftruction*, which led him into a wide field full of dark Mountains, where he ftumbled and fell, and rife no more.

[h] *The dan- ger of turning out of the way.*

I looked then after *Chriftian*, to fee him go up the Hill, where I perceived he fell from running to going, and from going to clambering upon his hands and his knees, becaufe of the fteepnefs of the place. Now about the midway to the top of the Hill, was a pleafant [i] *Arbour*, made by the Lord of the Hill, for the refrefh- ment of weary Travailers. Thither therefore *Chriftian* got, where alfo

[i] *A ward of grace.*

he

he fat down to reft him. Then he
pull'd his Roll out of his bofom and
read therein to his comfort; he alfo
now began afrefh to take a review
of the Coat or Garment that was
given him as he ftood by the Crofs.
Thus pleafing himfelf a while, he at
laft fell into a flumber, and thence
into a faft fleep, which detained him
in that place untill it was almoft
night, and in his fleep his ¹ Roll fell
out of his hand. Now as he was fleeping, there came one to him & awaked
him faying, *Go to the Ant, thou flug-
gard, confider her ways and be wife*:
and with that *Chriftian* fuddenly ftar-
ted up, and fped him on his way,
and went a pace till he came to the
top of the Hill.

marginal note: ¹ *He that fleeps is a lofer.*

Now when he was got up to the
top of the Hill, there came two Men
running againft him amain; the name
of the one was *Timorus*, and the name
of the other *Miftruft*. To whom
Chriftian faid, Sirs, what's the matter
you run the wrong way? *Timorus*
anfwered, That they were going to
the City of *Zion*, and had got up
that *difficult* place; but, faid he, the
further we go, the more danger we
meet

... whereupon we turned, and
... going back again.

... said *Mistrust*, for just before
... lye a couple of Lyons in the
... , whether sleeping or wake-
ing we know not; and we could not
think , if we came within reach, but
they would presently pull us in pieces.

Chr. Then said *Christian*, You make
me afraid, but whither shall I fly to
be safe? If I go back to mine own
Countrey, *That* is prepared for Fire
and Brimstone ; and I shall certainly
perish there. If I can get to the Coelestial City, I am sure to be in safety
there. I must venture : To go back
is nothing but death, to go forward
is fear of death, and life everlasting
beyond it. I will yet go forward. So
Mistrust and *Timorus* ran down
the Hill ; and *Christian* went on his
way. But thinking again of what he
heard from the men, he felt in his bosom for his Roll, that he might read
therein and be comforted ; but he
felt and ᵏ found it not. Then was *Chri-*
stian in great distress , and knew not
what to do, for he wanted that which
used to relieve him, and that which
should have been his Pass into the
Coelestial

ᵏ Christian
missed his
Roll,
wherein he
used to
take Com-
fort.

leftial City. Here therefore he began to be much perplexed, and knew not what to do ; at laft he bethought himfelf that he had flept in the *Arbour* that is on the fide of the Hill : and falling down upon his knees, he asked God forgivenefs for that his foolifh Fact ; and then went back to look for his Roll. But all the way he went back, who can fufficiently fet forth the forrow of *Chriftians* heart? fomtimes he fighed, fomtimes he wept, and often times he chid himfelf, for being fo foolifh to fall afleep in that place which was erected only for a little refrefhment from his wearinefs. Thus therefore he went back; carefully looking on this fide, and on that, all the way as he went, if happily he might find his Roll, that had been his comfort fo many times in his Journey. He went thus till he came again within fight of the *Arbour*, where he fat and flept; but that fight renew-

Chriftian bewails his foolifh fleeping.
Rev. 2. 2.

ed [1]his forrow the more, by bringing again, even a frefh, his evil of fleeping into his mind. Thus therefore he now went on bewailing his finful fleep, faying, *O wretched man that I am,* that I should sleep in the day, that I should sleep in the midst of difficulty! that I should so indulge my flesh, as to use that rest for ease to my flesh, which the Lord of the Hill hath erected only for the relief of the spirits of Pilgrims! How many steps have I took in vain! (Thus it happened to *Israel* for their sin, they were sent back again by the way of the Red-Sea) and I am made to tread those steps with sorrow, which I might have trod with delight, had it not been for this sinful sleep. How far might I have been on my way by this time! I am made to tread those steps thrice over, which I needed not to have trod but once: Yea now also I am like to be benighted, for the day is almost spent. O that I had not slept! Now by this time he was come to the *Arbour* again, where for a while he sat down and wept, but at last (as *Christian* would have it) looking sorrowfully down under the Settle, there he espied his Roll; the which he with trembling and haste catch't up, and put it into his bosom; but who can tell how joyful this Man was, when he had gotten his Roll a-gain!

gain ! For this Roll was the affurance
of his life and acceptance at the defired Haven.   Therefore he laid it
up in his bofom, gave thanks to God
for directing his eye to the place
where it lay , and with joy and tears
betook him felf again to his Journey.
But Oh how nimbly now, did he go
up the reft of the Hill ! Yet before
he got up, the Sun went down upon
Chriftian; and this made him again
recall the vanity of his fleeping to his
remembrance, and thus he again began to condole with himfelf : *Ah thou*
finful fleep ! how for thy fake am I like to
be benighted in my Journey !   I muft
walk without the Sun , darknefs muft
cover the path of my feet, and I muft
bear the noife of doleful Creatures , be-
caufe of my finful fleep ! Now alfo he
remembered the ftory that *Miftruft*
and *Timorus* told him of, how they
were frighted with the fight of the
Lions.   Then faid *Chriftian* to himfelf again, Thefe Beafts range in the
night for their prey, and if they fhould
meet with me in the dark, how fhould
I fhift them ! how fhould I efcape being by them torn pieces ?   Thus he
went on his way, but while he was
thus

... his unhappy miscar-
... he lift up his eyes, and behold
... was a very stately Palace be-
... him, the name whereof was
... , and it stood just by the
... way side.

So I saw in my Dream, that he
made haste and went forward, that if
possible hemight get Lodging there;
now before he had gone far, he entred into a very narrow passage,
which was about a furlong off of the
Porters Lodge, and looking very
narrowly before him as he went, he
espied two Lions in the way. Now,
thought he, I see the dangers that
Misdrust and *Timorus*, were driven
back by. (The Lions were Chained,
but he saw not the Chains) Then he
was afraid, and thought also himself
to go back after them, for he thought
nothing but death was before him:
But the *Porter* at the Lodge, whose
Name is ᵐ *Watchful*, perceiving that m Mar. 53
Christian made a halt, as if he would
go back, cried unto him, saying,
Is thy strength so small? fear not the
Lions, for they are Chained: and are
placed there for trial of faith where it
is; and for discovery of those that
have

have none : keep in the midſt of the Path, and no hurt ſhall come unto thee.

Then I ſaw that he went on, trembling for fear of the Lions ; but taking good heed to the directions of the *Porter*; he heard them roar, but they did him no harm. Then he clapt his hands, and went on, till he came and ſtood before the Gate where the *Porter* was. Then ſaid *Chriſtian* to the *Porter*, Sir, What houſe is this? and may I lodge here to night? The *Porter* anſwered, This Houſe was built by the Lord of the Hill: and he built it for the relief and ſecurity of Pilgrims. The *Porter* alſo asked whence he was, and whither he was going?

Chr. I am come from the City of *Deſtruction*, and am going to Mount *Zion*, but becauſe the Sun is now ſet, I deſire, if I may, to lodge here to night.

Por. *What is your name?*

Chr. My name is now *Chriſtian*; but my name at the firſt was *Graceleſs:* I came of the Race of *Japhet*, whom God will perſwade to dwell in the Tents of *Shem.*

Por.

... it ... to happen that you ... late, the Sun is set?

Chr. I had been here sooner, but that, wretched man that I am! I slept in the *Arbour* that stands on the Hill side; nay, I had notwithstanding that, been here much sooner, but that in my sleep I lost my Evidence, and came without it to the brow of the Hill; and then feeling for it, and finding it not, I was forced with sorrow of heart, to go back to the place where I slept my sleep, where I found it, and now I am come.

Por. Well, I will call out one of the Virgins of this place, who will, if she likes your talk, bring you in to the rest of the Family, according to the Rules of the House. So *Watchful* the *Porter* rang a Bell, at the sound of which, came out at the door of the House, a Grave and Beautiful Damsel, named *Discretion*, and asked why she was called.

The *Porter* answered, This Man is in a Journey from the City of *Destruction* to Mount *Zion*, but being weary, and benighted, he asked me if he might lodge here to night; so I told him I would call for thee, who

after

after difcourfe had with him, mayeſt do as feemeth thee good, even according to the Law of the Houfe.

Then fhe asked him whence he was, and whither he was going, and he told her. She asked him alfo, how he got into the way, and he told her; Then fhe asked him, What he had feen, and met with in the way, and he told her; and laft, fhe asked his name, fo he faid, It is *Chriſtian*; and I have fo much the more a defire to lodge here to night, becaufe, by what I perceive, this place was built by the Lord of the Hill, for the relief and fecurity of Pilgrims. So fhe fmiled, but the water ſtood in her eyes: And after a little paufe, fhe faid, I will call forth two or three more of the Family. So fhe ran to the door, and called out *Prudence*, *Piety*, and *Charity*, who after a little more difcourfe with him, had him in to the Family; and many of them meeting him at the threfhold of the Houfe, faid, Come in thou bleffed of the Lord; this Houfe was built by the Lord of the Hill, on purpofe to entertain fuch Pilgrims in. Then he bowed his head, and followed
ed

the House. So when he was come in, and set down, they gave him somthing to drink; and consented together that until supper was ready, some one or two of them should have some particular discourse with *Christian*, for the best improvement of time: and they appointed *Piety*, and *Prudence*, to discourse with him; and thus they began.

Piety. Come good Christian, *since we have been so loving to you, to receive you into our House this night; let us, if perhaps we may better our selves thereby, talk with you of all things that have happened to you in your Pilgrimage.*

Chr. With a very good will, and I am glad that you are so well disposed.

Piety What moved you at first to betake yourself to a Pilgrims life.

Chr. I was ª driven out of my Native Countrey, by a dreadful sound that was in mine ears, to wit, That unavoidable destruction did attend me, if I abode in that place where I was.

Piety. *But how did it happen that you came out of your Countrey this way?*

ª How Christian was driven out of his own Countrey.

Chr. It was as God would have it, for when I was under the fears of destruction, I did not know whither to go; but by chance there came a Man, even to me, (as I was trembling and weeping) whose name is b *Evangelist*, and he directed me to the Wicket-Gate, which else I should never have found; and so set me into the way that hath led me directly to this House.

b *How he get into the Way to Sion.*

Piety. *But did you not come by the House of the Interpreter?*

Chr. Yes, and did see such things there, the remembrance of which will stick by me as long as I live; specially three c things, *to wit,* How Christ, in despite of Satan, maintains his work of Grace in the heart; how the Man had sinned himself quite out of hopes of Gods mercy; and also the Dream of him that thought in his sleep the day of Judgement was come.

c *A reherfal of what he faw in the way.*

Piety. *Why? Did you hear him tell his Dream?*

Chr. Yes, and a dreadful one it was. I thought it made my heart ake as he was telling of it, but yet I am glad I heard it.

Piety.

_____ you saw at
_____ the Interpreter?

_____ he took me and had
_____ where he shewed me a stately
_____, and how the People were
_____ in Gold that were in it; and
_____ there came a venturous Man,
_____ cut his way through the armed
_____ that stood in the door to keep
_____ out; and how he was bid to come
in, and win eternal Glory. Methought
those things did ravish my heart; I
could have staid at that good Mans
house a twelve-month, but that I
knew I had further to go.

*Piety. And what saw you else in the
way?*

Chr. Saw! Why I went but a little
further, and I saw one, as I thought
in my mind, hang bleeding upon the
Tree; and the very sight of him made
my burden fall off my back (for I
groaned under a weary burden) but
then it fell down from off me. 'Twas
a strange thing to me, for I never saw
such a thing before: Yea, and while
I stood looking up, (for then I could
not forbear looking) three shining
ones came to me: one of them testi-
fied that my sins were forgiven me;

another

another ſtript me of my Rags, and gaveme this Broidred Coat which you ſee; and the third ſet the mark which you ſee, in my forehead, and gave me this ſealed Roll (and with that he plucked it out of his boſom.)

Piety. *But you ſaw more then this, did you not?*

Chr. The things that I have told you were the beſt: yet ſome other ſmall matters I ſaw, as namely I ſaw three Men, *Simple, Sloth,* and *Preſumption,* lye a ſleep a little out of the way as I came, with Irons upon their heels; but do you think I could awake them! I alſo ſaw *Formaliſt* and *Hypocriſie* come tumbling over the wall, to go, as they pretended, to *Sion,* but they were quickly loſt; even as I my ſelf did tell them, but they would not believe: but, above all, I found it *hard* work to get up this Hill, and as *hard* to come by the Lions mouths; and truly if it had not been for the good Man, the Porter that ſtands at the Gate, I do not know, but that after all, I might have gone back again: but now I thank God I am here, and I thank you for receiving of me.

Then

Pru. *Do you not think somtimes of the Countrey from whence you came?*

Chr. Yes,[d] but with much shame and detestation; *Truly, if I had been mindful of that Countrey from whence I came out, I might have had opportuni-ty to have returned, but now I desire a better Countrey, that is, an Heavenly.*

Pru. Do you not yet bear away with you some of the things that then you were conversant withal?

Chr. Yes, but greatly against my will; especially my inward and [*]carnal cogitations; with which all my Countrey-men, as well as my self, were delighted; but now all those things are my grief: and might I but chuse mine own things, I would [f]chuse never to think of those things more; but when I would be doing of that which is best, that which is worst is with me.

Pru. Do you not find sometimes, as if those things were vanquished, which at other times are your perplexity.

Chr. Yes, but that is but seldom;

d Christians thoughts of his Native Countrey. Heb. 11. 15, 16.

e Christian disgusted with carnal cogitations.

f Christians choice.

g Chri-
stians gol-
den hours. but they are to me *Golden hours,
in which such things happens to
me.

    Pru. *Can you remember by what
means you find your anoyances at times,
as if they were vanquished?*

h How
Christian
gets power
against his
corrupti-
ons.   *Chr.* Yes, when [h] I think what I
saw at the Cross, that will do it; and
when I look upon my Broidered
Coat, that will do it; also when I
look into the Roll that I carry in my
bosom, that will do it; and when
my thoughts wax warm about whi-
·ther I am going, that will do it.

    Pru. *And what is it that makes you
so desirous to go to Mount* Zion?

i Why
Christian
would be
at Mount
Zion.   *Chr.* Why, [i] there I hope to see
him *alive*, that did hang *dead* on the
Cross; and there I hope to be
rid of all those things, that to this
day are in me, an anoiance to me;
there they say there is no death, and
there I shall dwell with such Company as I like best. For to tell you
truth, I love him, because I was by him
eased of my burden, and I am weary
of my inward sickness; I would fain
be where I shall die no more, and
with the Company that shall continually cry *Holy, Holy, Holy.*

    Now I saw in my Dream, that thus
they

...talking together until supper was ready. So when they had [...] ready, they sat down to meat; and the Table was furnished [k] with [...] things, and with Wine that was well refined; and all their talk [l] at the Table, was about the Lord of the Hill: As namely, about what he had done, and wherefore he did what he did, and why he had builded that House: and by what they said, I perceived that he had been a *great Warriour*, and had fought with and slain him that had the power of death, but not without great danger to himself, which made me love him the more.

For, as they said, and as I believe (said *Christian*) he did it with the loss of much blood; but that which put Glory of Grace into all he did, was, that he did it of pure love to his Countrey. And besides, there were some of them of the Household that said, they had seen and spoke with him since he did dye on the Cross; and they have attested, that they had it from his own lips, that he is such a lover of poor Pilgrims,

that

k *What Christian had to his supper.*

l *Their talk at supper time.*

that the like is not to be found from the East to the West.

They moreover gave an instance of what they affirmed, and that was, He had stript himself of his glory that he might do this for the Poor ; and that they heard him say and affirm, That he would not dwell in the Mountain of *Zion* alone.   They said moreover, That he had made many Pilgrims ^a Princes, though by nature they were Beggars born, and their original had been the Dunghil.

a Christ makes Princes of Beggars.

Thus they difcoursed together till late at night, and after they had committed themfelves to their Lord for Protection , they betook themfelves to reft.   The Pilgrim they laid in a large upper ^b Chamber, whofe window opened towards the Sun rifing ; the name of the Chamber was *Peace*, where he flept till break of day ; and then he awoke and fang,

Chriftians Bed-chamber.

Where am I now ! is this the love and care
Of Jefus, for the men that Pilgrims are !
Thus to provide ! That I should be forgiven !
And dwell already the next door to
Heaven.   So

[... Morning] they all got up, [and after] some more discourse, they [would] him that he should not depart, [till] they had shewed him the *Rarities* [of that] place. And first they had him [into] the Study, ^c where they shew-ed him Records of the greatest Anti-quity; in which, as I remember my Dream, they shewed him first the Pedigree of the Lord of the Hill, that he was the Son of the Ancient of Days, and came by an eternal Generation. Here also was more fully Recorded the Acts that he had done, and the names of many hun-dreds that he had taken into his service; and how he had placed them in such Habitations that could nei-ther by length of Days nor decaies of Nature, be dissolved.

Then they read to him some of the worthy Acts that some of his Ser-vants had done. As how they had subdued Kingdoms, wrought Righte-ousness, obtained Promises, stopped the mouths of Lions, quenched the ^dviolence of Fire, escaped the edge of the Sword; out of weakness were made strong, waxed valiant in fight, and turned to flight the Ar-mies of the *Aliens*.   Then

Then they read again in another part of the Records of the House, where it was shewed how willing their Lord was to receive into his favour any, even any, though they in time past had offered great affronts to his Person and proceedings. Here also were several other Histories of many other famous things, of all which *Christian* had a view. As of things both Ancient and Modern; together with Prophecies and Predictions of things that have their certain accomplishment, both to the dread and amazement of enemies, and the comfort and solace of Pilgrims.

The next day they took him and had him into the ª Armory; where they shewed him all manner of Furniture, which their Lord had provided for Pilgrims, as Sword, Shield, Helmet, Brest plate, *All-Prayer*, and Shooes that would not wear out. And there was here enough of this to harness out as many men for the service of their Lord, as there be Stars in the Heaven for multitude.

e Christian had into the Armory.

They

[...] him fome of the
[...] with which fome of his Ser-
[...] had done wonderful things.
[...] hey fhewed him *Mofes* Rod, the f *Chriftian*
[...]mmer and Nail with which *Jael* *is made to*
[...] *Sifera*, the Pitchers, Trumpets, *fee Ancient*
[...] Lamps too, with which *Gideon* *things.*
[...] to flight the Armies of *Midian*.
Then they fhewed him the Oxes goad
wherewith *Shamger* flew fix hundred
men. They fhewed him alfo the
Jaw bone with which *Sampfon* did
fuch mighty feats; they fhewed him
moreover the Sling and Stone with
which *David* flew *Goliab* of *Gath*:
and the Sword alfo with which their
Lord will kill the Man of Sin, in the
day that he fhall rife up to the prey.
They fhewed him befides many excellent things, with which *Chriftian*
was much delighted. This done, they
went to their reft again.

• Then I faw in my Dream, that on
the morrow he got up to go forwards,
but they defired him to ftay till the
next day alfo and then faid they, we
will, if the day be clear, fhew you the
* delectable Mountains; which they g *Chriftian*
faid, would yet furtheradd to his com- *fhewed the*
fort; becaufe they were nearer the *delectable*
de- *Mountains*

desired Haven, then the place where at present he was. So he consented and staid. When the Morning was up, they had him to the top of the House, h and bid him look South, so he did; and behold at a great distance he saw a most pleasant Mountainous Countrey, beautified with Woods, Vinyards, Fruits of all sorts, Flowers also; Springs and Fountains, very delectable to behold. Then he asked the name of the Countrey, they said it was *Immanuels Land*: and it is as common, said they, as this *Hill* is, to and for all the Pilgrims. And when thou comest there, from thence, said they, thou maist see to the Gate of the Cœlestial City, as the Shepheards that live there will make appear.

Now he bethought himself of setting forward, i and they were willing he should: but first, said they, let us go again into the Armory, so they did; and when he came there, they k harnessed him from head to foot, with what was of proof, lest perhaps he should meet with assaults in the way. He being therefore thus a-coutred walketh out with his friends

to

h Isa. 35. 26, 27.

Christian sets forward.

k *Christian sent away Armed.*

.... where he asked the
.... any Pilgrims pass by
.... the *Porter* answered, Yes.

.... Pray did you know him?

.... I asked his name, and he
.... me it was *Faithful.*

.... *Chr.* O, said *Christian*, I know
him, he is my Towns-man, my near
Neighbour, he comes from the place
where I was born : how far do you
think he may be before?

Porter. He is got by this time below the Hill.

Chr. Well, said *Christian*, good
Porter the Lord be with thee, and add
to all thy blessings much increase, for
the kindness that thou hast shewed
to me.

1 How
Christian
and the
Porter
greet at
parting.

Then he began to go forward, but
Discretion, *Piety*, *Charity*, and *Prudence*, would accompany him down
to the foot of the Hill. So they went
on together, reiterating their former
discourses till they came to go down
the Hill. Then said *Christian*, As it
was *difficult* coming up, so (so far as
I can see) it is *dangerous* going down.
Yes, said *Prudence*, so it is; for it is an
hard matter for a man to go down
into the valley of *Humiliation*, as
thou

thou art now, and to catch no flip by
the way; therefore, said they, are
we come out to accompany thee
down the Hill. So he began to go
down, but very warily, yet he caught
a flip or too.

Then I faw in my Dream, that
thefe good Companions, when *Chriftian* was gone down to the bottom of
the Hill, gave him a loaf of Bread,
a bottle of Wine, and a clufter of
Raifins; and then he went on his
way.

But now in this Valley of *Humiliation* poor *Chriftian* was hard put
to it, for he had gone but a little way
before he efpied a foul *Fiend* coming over the field to meet him; his
name is *Apollyon*. Then did *Chriftian* begin to be afraid, and to caft
in his mind whither to go back, or to
ftand his ground. But he confidered
again, that he had no Armour for
his back, and therefore thought that
to turn the back to him, might give
him greater advantage with eafe to
*Chriftians pierce him with his Darts; there-
refolution fore he refolved* k *to venture, and
at the ap- ftand his ground. For thought he,
preach of had I no more in mine eye, then the
Apollyon* saving

... would be the best ...

... went on, and *Apollyon* met ... now the Monster was hidious ... behold, he was cloathed with ... like a Fish (and they are his ... he had Wings like a Dragon, ... out of his belly came Fire and ... mouth, and his mouth was as the ... mouth of a Lion. When he was ... come up to *Christian*, he beheld him ... with a disdainful countenance, and ... thus began to question with him.

Apol. *Whence come you and whither are you bound?*

Chr. I come from the City of Destruction, [1] which is the place of all evil, and am going to the City of Zion.

1 *Discourse betwixt* Christian *and Apollyon.*

Apol. *By this I perceive thou art one of my Subjects, for all that Country is mine; and I am the Prince and God of it. How is it then that thou hast ran away from thy King? Were it not that I hope thou maiest do me more service, I would strike thee now at one blow to the ground.*

Chr. I was born indeed in your Dominions, but your service was hard, and your wages such as a man could

could not live on, *for the Wages of Sin is death*; therefore when I was come to years, I did as other confiderate perfons do, look out, if perhaps I might mend my felf,

Apol. There is no Prince that will thus lightly lofe his Subjects; neither will I as yet lofe thee. But fince thou complaineft of thy fervice and wages ᵐ *be* ᵐ Apolly-*content to go back; what our Countrey* ons flatte-*will afford, I do here promife to give* ry. *thee.*

Chr. But I have let my felf to another, even to the King of Princes, and how can I with fairnefs go back with thee?

Apol. Thou haft done in this, accor- ⁿApollyon*ding to the Proverb,* ᵘ *changed a* underva-*bad for a worfe: but it is ordinary for* lues Chrifts *thofe that have profeffed themfelves his* fervice. *Servants, after a while to give him the flip, and return again to me: do thou fo to, and all fhall be well.*

Chr. I have given him my faith, and fworn my Allegiance to him; how then can I go back from this, and not be hanged as a Traitor?

Apol. Thou dideft the fame to me, Apollyon o *and yet I am willing to pafs by all, if* pretends to *now thou will turn again, and go back.* be merciful

Chr.

... ... then was
... ... and besides, I
... ... the Prince under whose
... now I stand, is able to ab-
... me; yea, and to pardon also
... I did as to my compliance with
... and besides, (O thou destroy-
ing Apollyon) to speak truth, I like
his Service, his Wages, his Servants,
his Government, his Company, and
Countrey better then thine: and
therefore leave off to perswade me
further, I am his Servant, and I will
follow him.

Apol. *Consider again when thou art
in cool blood, what thou art like to meet
with in the way that thou goest. Thou
knowest that for the most part, his Servants come to an ill end, because they are
transgressors against me, and my ways:
How many of them have been put to
shameful deaths! and besides, thou coun-
test his service better then mine, whereas
he never came yet from the place where
he is, to deliver any that served him
out of our hands: but as for me, how
many times, as all the World very well
knows, have I delivered, either by
power or fraud, those that have faithfully served me, from him and his,*

Apollyon
pleads the
grievous
ends of
Christians
to disswade
Christian
from per-
sisting in
his way.

though taken by them, and so I will
deliver them.

Chr. His forbearing at present to
deliver them, is on purpose to try
their love, whether they will cleave
to him to the end : and as for the ill
end thou sayest they come too, that
is most glorious in there account: For
for present deliverance, they do not
much expect it; for they stay for
their Glory, and then they shall have
it, when their Prince comes in his,
and the Glory of the Angels.

*Apol. Thou hast already been un-
faithful in thy service to him, and how
dost thou think to receive wages of
him ?*

Chr. Wherein, O *Apollyon,* have
I been unfaithful to him.

*Apol. Thou didst faint at first
setting out, when thou wast almost
choked in the Gulf of Dispond. Thou
diddest attempt wrong ways to be rid of
thy burden whereas thou shouldest have
stayed till thy Prince had taken it off:
Thou didst sinfully sleep and loose thy
choice thing : thou wast also almost perswaded to go back, at the sight of the
Lions ; and when thou talkest of thy
Journey, and of what thou hast heard,
and*

Apollyon pleads Christians infirmities against him.

...rdly defirous of
... all that thou fayeft or

Chr. All this is true, and much
more, which thou haft left out ; but
the Prince whom I ferve and honour, is merciful, and ready to forgive: but befides, thefe infirmities
poffeffed me in thy Countrey, for
there I fuckt them in, and I have
groaned under them, been forry for
them, and have obtained pardon of
my Prince.

Apol. Then *Apollyon* broke out in- Apollyon
to a grievous rage, faying, *I am an* in a rage
Enemy to this Prince : I hate his Per- falls upon
fon, his Laws, and People : I am come Chriftian.
out on purpofe to withftand thee.

Chr. *Apollyon* beware what you
do, for I am in the Kings High-way,
the way of Holinefs , therefore take
heed to your felf.

Apol. Then *Apollyon* ftrodled quite
over the whole breadth of the way,
and faid, I am void of fear in this
matter, prepare thyfelf to dye, for
I fwear thou fhalt go no further, here
will I fpill thy foul ; and with that,
he threw a flaming Dart at his breft,
but *Chriftian* had a Shield in his hand,

with which he caught it, and so prevented the danger of that. Then did *Christian* draw, for he saw 'twas time to bestir him; and *Apollyon* as fast made at him, throwing Darts as thick as Hail; by the which, notwithstanding all that *Christian* could do to avoid it, *Apollyon* wounded him in his head, his hand and foot; this made *Christian* give a little back: *Apollyon* therefore followed his work amain, and *Christian* again took courage, and resisted as manfully as he could. This sore Combat lasted for above half a day, even till *Christian* was almost quite spent. For you must know that *Christian* by reason of his wounds, must needs grow weaker and weaker.

Christian wounded in his understanding, faith and conversation.

Then *Apollyon* espying his opportunity, began to gather up close to *Christian*, and wrestling with him, gave him a dreadful fall; and with that, *Christians* Sword flew out of his hand. Then said *Apollion, I am sure of thee now*; and with that, he had almost prest him to death, so that *Christian* began to despair of life. But as God would have it, while *Apollyon* was fetching of his last blow, there-

Apollyon casteth down to the ground the Christian.

...made a full end of this ...combat, Christian nimbly reached ...his hand for his Sword, and ...caught it, saying, *Rejoyce not against me, O mine Enemy! when I fall, I shall arise;* and with that, gave him a deadly thruft, which made him give back, as one that had received his mortal wound: *Christian* perceiving that, made at him again, saying, *Nay, in all thefe things we are more then Conquerours.* And with that, *Apollyon* fpread forth his Dragons wings, and fped him away, that *Chriftian* for a feafon faw him no more.

In this combat no man can imagine, unlefs he had feen and heard as I did, what yelling, and hideous roaring *Apollyon* made all the time of the fight, he fpake like a Dragon: and on the other fide, what fighs and groans braft from *Chriftians* heart. I never faw him all the while, give fo much as one pleafant look, till he perceived he had wounded *Apollyon* with his two edged Sword, then indeed he did fmile, and look upward: but 'twas the dreadfulleft fight that ever I faw.

Chriftians victory over Apollyon.

Jam. 4. 7.

A brief relation of the Combat by the fpectator.

F 3   So

Christian gives God thanks for deliverances.

So when the Battel was over, Christian said, I will here give thanks to him that hath delivered me out of the mouth of the Lion; to him that did help me against Apollyon: and so he did, saying,

Great Beelzebub, the Captain of this Fiend,
Design'd my ruin; therefore to this end
He sent him harneft out, and he with rage
That Hellish was, did fiercely me Ingage:
But blessed Michael helped me, and I
By dint of Sword did quickly make him flye;
Therefore to him let me give lasting praise,
And thank and bless his holy name always.

Then there came to him an hand, with some of the leaves of the Tree of Life, the which Christian took, and applyed to the wounds that he had received in the Battel, and was healed immediately. He also sat down in that place to eat Bread, and to drink of the Bottle that was given him

little . . . ; so being refresh-
. . . . addressed himself to his Jour-
. . . with his [a] Sword drawn in his
. . . , for he said, I know not but
some other Enemy may be at hand.
But he met with no other affront
from *Apollyon*, quite through this
Valley.

[a] *Christian goes on his Journey with his Sword drawn in his hand.*

Now at the end of this Valley, was
another, called the Valley of the
Shadow of Death, and *Christian* must
needs go through it, because the
way to the Cœlestial City lay
through the midst of it: Now this
Valley is a very solitary place. The
Prophet [b] *Jeremiah* thus describes it,
*A Wilderness, a Land of desarts, and
of Pits, a Land of drought, and of the
shadow of death, a Land that no Man
(but a Christian) passeth through, and
where no man dwelt.*

[b] Jer. 2. 6.

Now here *Christian* was worse
put to it then in his fight with *Apollyon*, as by the sequel you shall see.

I saw then in my Dream, that
when *Christian* was got to the Borders
of the Shadow of Death, there
met him two Men, [c] Children of
them that brought up an evil report
of the good Land, making haste to

[c] *The children of the Spies go back.*

go

go back: to whom *Christian* spake as follows.

Chr. *Whither are you going?*

Men. They said, Back, back ; and would have you to do so too, if either life or peace is prized by you.

Chr. *Why? whats the matter? said* Christian.

Men. Matter! said they; we were going that way as you are going, and went as far as we durst ; and indeed we were almost past coming back, for had we gone alittle further, we had not been here to bring the news to thee.

Chr. *But what have you met with, said* Christian ?

Men. Why we were almost in the Valley of the shadow of death, but that by good hap we looked before us, and saw the danger before we came to it.

Psal. 44. 19. Psal. 107. 10.

Chr. *But what have you seen, said* Christian ?

Men. Seen ! why the valley it self, which is as dark as pitch; we also saw there the Hobgoblins, Satyrs, and Dragons of the Pit: we heard also in that Valley a continual howling and yelling, as of a people under
der

... misery ; who there ... in affliction and Irons: and ... that Valley hangs the discou- d Job. 3.5. ch. 10. 22. ... ing [d] Clouds of confusion, death ... doth always spread his wings ... it : in a word, it is every whit ... dreadful, being utterly without Order.

Chr. Then said Christian, *I per-ceive not yet, by what you have said, but that* [e] *this is my way to the desired* e Jer. 2.6 *Haven.*

Men. Be it thy way, we will not chuse it for ours; so they parted, and *Christian* went on his way, but still with his Sword drawn in his hand, for fear left he should be assaulted.

I saw then in my Dream, so far as Ps. 69. 14 this Valley reached, there was on the right hand a very deep Ditch; That Ditch is it into which the blind have led the blind in all Ages, and have both there miserably perished. Again, behold on the left hand, there was a very dangerous Quagg, into which, if even a good Man falls, he can find no botttom for his foot to stand on; Into that Quagg *King Da-vid once did fall*, and had no doubt therein been smothered, had not He that is able, pluckt him out.

The

The path-way was here also exceeding narrow, and therefore good *Christian* was the more put to it; for when he sought in the dark to shun the ditch on the one hand, he was ready to tip over into the mire on the other; also when he sought to escape the mire, without great carefulness he would be ready to fall into the ditch. Thus he went on, and I heard him here sigh bitterly: for besides the dangers mentioned above, the path-way was here so dark, that oft times when he lift up his foot to set forward, he knew not where, or upon what he should set it next.

About the midst of this Valley, I perceived the mouth of Hell to be, and it stood also hard by the way side: Now thought *Christian*, what shall I do? And ever and anon the flame and smoak would come out in such abundance, with sparks and hideousnoises, (things that cared not for *Christians* Sword, as did *Apollyon* before) that he was forced to put up his Sword, and betake himself to another weapon called f *All-prayer*, so he cried in my hearing, g *O Lord I beseech thee deliver my Soul*. Thus he went

f Eph 6. 18
Pl. 116. 3.

... a good while, yet still the
... should be reaching towards
... also he heard doleful voices, and
...things too and fro, so that sometimes he thought he should be torn in
pieces, or troden down like mire in
the Streets. This frightful sight was
seen, and these dreadful noises were
heard by him for several miles toge- Christian
put to a
ther : and coming to a place, where
he thought he heard a company of stand, but
for a while
Fiends coming forward to meet him,
he stopt, and began to muse what he
had best to do. Somtimes he had
half a thought to go back. Then
again he thought he might be half
way through the Valley; he remembred also how he had already vanquished many a danger : and that
the danger of going back might be
much more, then for to go forward,
so he resolved to go on. Yet the
Fiends seemed to come nearer and
nearer, but when they were come
even almost at him, he cried out
with a most vehement voice , *I will*
walk in the strength of the Lord God ;
so they gave back, and came no further.

One thing I would not let slip, I
took

took notice that now poor *Christian* was so confounded, that he did not know his own voice: and thus I perceived it : Just when he was come over against the mouth of the burning Pit, one of the wicked ones got behind him, and stept up softly to him, and whisperingly suggested many grievous blasphemies to him, which he *a* verily thought had proceeded from his own mind. This put *Christian* more to it than any thing that he met with before, even to think that he should now blaspheme him that he loved so much before; yet could he have helped it, he would not have done it : but he had not the discretion neither to stop his ears, nor to know from whence those blasphemies came.

a Christian made believe that he spake blasphemies, when 'twas Satan that suggested them into his mind.

When *Christian* had travelled in this disconsolate condition some considerable time, he thought he heard the voice of a man, as going before him, saying, *Though I walk through the valley of the shaddow of death, I will fear none ill, for thou art with me.*

Pf. 23. 4.

Then was he glad, and that for these reasons :

First, Because he gathered from
thence

... that ſome who feared God
... in this Valley as well as himſelf.
... Secondly, For that he perceived
God was with them, though in that
dark and diſmal ſtate; and why not,
thought he, with me, though by reaſon Job 9. 11.
of the impediment that attends this
place, I cannot perceive it.

Thirdly, For that he hoped (could
he over-take them) to have compa-
ny by and by. So he went on, and Amos 5. 8.
called to him that was before, but he
knew not what to anſwer, for that he
thought himſelf to be alone: And by
and by, the day broke; then ſaid *Chriſtian, He hath turned the ſhadow of
death into the morning.*   Chriſtian

Now morning being come, he look- *glad at*
ed back, not of deſire to return, but *break of*
to ſee, by the light of the day, what *day.*
hazards he had gone through in the
dark. So he ſaw more perfectly the
Ditch that was on the one hand, and
the Quag that was on the other; alſo how narrow the way was which
lay betwixt them both; alſo now he
ſaw the Hobgoblins, and Satyrs, and
Dragons of the Pit, but all afar off,
for after break of day, they came not
nigh; yet they were diſcovered to
                              him

him, according to that which is written, *He discovereth deep things out of darkness, and bringeth out to light the shadow of death.*

Now was *Christian* much affected with his deliverance from all the dangers of his solitary way, which dangers, tho he feared them more before, yet he saw them more clearly now, becaufe the light of the day made them conspicuous to him; and about this time the Sun was rifing, and this was another mercy to *Christian*: for you muft note, that tho the firft part of the Valley of the Shadow of death was dangerous, yet this fecond part which he was yet to go, was, if poffible, far more dangerous: for from the place where he now ftood, even to the end of the Valley, the way was all along fet fo full of Snares, Traps, Gins, and Nets here, and fo full of Pits, Pitfalls, deep holes and fhelvings down there, that had it now been dark, as it was when he came the firft part of the way, had he had a thoufand fouls, they had in reafon been caft away; but as I faid, juft now the Sun was rifing. Then faid he, *His candle fhineth on my head*

Job 29. 2.

In this light therefore, he came to the end of the Valley. Now I faw in my Dream, that at the end of this Valley lay blood, bones, afhes, and mangled bodies of men, even of Pilgrims that had gone this way formerly: And while I was mufing what fhould be the reafon, I efpied alittle before me a Cave, where two Giants, *Pope* and *Pagan*, dwelt in old time, by whofe Power and Tyranny the Men whofe bones, blood, afhes, &c. lay there, were cruelly put to death. But by this place *Chriftian* went without much danger, whereat I fomewhat wondered; but I have learnt fince, that *Pagan* has been dead many a day; and as for the other, though he be yet alive, he is by reafon of age, and alfo of the many fhrewd brufhes that he met with in his younger dayes, grown fo crazy, and ftiff in his joynts, that he can now do little more then fit in his Caves mouth, grinning at Pilgrims as they go by, and biting his nails, becaufe he cannot come at them.

So I faw that *Chriftian* went on
his

his way, yet at the fight of the *old Man*, that fat in the mouth of the *Cave*, he could not tell what to think, ſpecially becauſe he ſpake to him, though he could not go after him; ſaying, *You will never mend, till more of you be burned*: but he held his peace, and ſet a good face on't, and ſo went by, and catcht no hurt. Then ſang *Chriſtian*,

O world of wonders! (I can ſay no leſs)
That I ſhould be preſerv'd in that di-ſtreſs
That I have met with here! O bleſſed bee
That band that from it hath delivered me!
Dangers in Darkneſs, Devils, Hell and Sin,
Did compaſs me, while I this Vale was in:
Yea, Snares, and Pits, and Traps, and Nets did lie
My path about, that worthleſs ſilly I
Might have been catch't, intangled,and caſt down:
But ſince I live, let JESUS wear the Crown.

Now

Christian went on his way,
... to a little afcent, which was
... up on purpofe, that Pilgrims
... fee before them: up there
... fore Christian went, and looking forward, he faw *Faithful* before
him, upon his Journey. Then faid
Christian aloud, Ho, ho, So-ho; ftay
and I will be your Companion. At
that *Faithful* looked behind him, to
whom *Christian* cried again, Stay,
ftay, till I come up to you: but *Faith-*
ful anfwered, *No*, I am upon my life,
and the Avenger of Blood is behind
me. At this *Christian* was fomwhat
moved, and putting to all his ftrength, *Christian*
he quickly got up with *Faithful*, and *overtakes*
did alfo over-run him, fo the *laft was* *Faithful.*
firft. Then did *Christian* vain-glo-
rioufly fmile, becaufe he had gotten
the ftart of his Brother: but not taking good heed to his feet, he fud- *Christian*
denly ftumbled and fell, and could *fall, makes*
not rife again, untill *Faithful* came up *Faithful*
to help him. *and he go*

  Then I faw in my Dream, they *lovingly*
went very lovingly on together; and *together*
had fweet difcourfe of all things that
had happened to them in their
Pilgrimage; and thus *Christian* began,   G   Chr.

Chr. My honoured and well beloved Brother Faithful, *I am glad that I have overtaken you; and that God has so tempered our spirits, that we can walk as Companions in this so pleasant a path.*

Fai. I had thought dear friend, to have had your company quite from our Town, but you did get the start of me; wherefore I was forced to come thus much of the way alone.

Chr. How long did you stay in the City of Destruction, *before you set out after me on your Pilgrimage?*

Fai. Till I could stay no longer; for there was great talk presently after you was gone out, that our City would in short time with Fire from Heaven be burned down to the ground.

Their talk about the Country from whence they came.

Chr. What! Did your Neighbours talk so?

Faith. Yes, 'twas for a while in every bodies mouth.

Chr. What, and did no more of them but you come out to escape the danger?

Faith. Though there was, as I said, a great talk thereabout, yet I do not think they did firmly believe it. For in the heat of the discourse

. . . . some of them deri-
. . . . . . speak of you, and of your
. . . . . . rate Journey, (for so they called
. . . your Pilgrimage) but I did believe, and do still, that the end of
our City will be with Fire and Brimstone from above: and therefore I
have made mine escape.

Chr. *Did you hear no talk of Neigh-*
bour Pliable?

Faith. Yes *Christian*, I heard that
he followed you till he came at the
Slough of *Dispond*; where, as some said,
he fell in; but he would not be
known to have so done: but I am sure
he was soundly bedabled with that
kind of dirt.

Chr. *And what said the Neighbours*
to him?

Faith. He hath since his going back
been had greatly in derision, and that
among all sorts of people: some do
mock and despise him, and scarce will
any set him on work. He is now seven
times worse then if he had never gone
out of the City.

How Ply-
able was
accounted
of when he
got home.

Chr. *But why should they be so set*
against him, since they also despise the
way that he forsook?

Faith. Oh, they fay, Hang him, he is a Turn-Coat, he was not true to his profeffion. I think God has ftired up even his Enemies to hifs at him, and make him a Proverb, becaufe he hath forfaken the way.

Jer.29.18, 29.

Chr. Had you no talk with him before you came out?

Faith. I met him once in the Streets, but he leered away on the other fide, as one afhamed of what he had done; fo I fpake not to him.

The Dog and Sow.

Chr. Well, at my firft fetting out, I had hopes of that Man; but now I fear he will perifh in the overthrow of the City, for it is happened to him, according to the true Proverb, The Dog is turned to his Vomit again, and the Sow that was Wafhed to her wallowing in the mire.

Faith. They are my fears of him too: But who can hinder that which will be?

Well Neighbour *Faithful*, faid *Chriftian*, let us leave him; and talk of things that more immediately concern our felves. *Tell me now, what you have met with in the way as you came; for I know you have met with*

fome

...th. I escaped the Slough that I ...ceive you fell into, and got up to the Gate without that danger; only I met with one whose name was *Wan-* *ton,* that had like to have done me a mischief.

Faithful *assaulted* by *Wan-ton.*

Chr. 'Twas well you escaped her *Net*; Joseph *was hard put to it by her, and be escaped her as you did, but it had like to have cost him his life. But what did she do to you?*

Faith. You cannot think (but that you know somthing) what a flattering tongue she had, she lay at me hard to turn aside with her, promising me all manner of content.

Chr. Nay, she did not promise you the content of a good conscience.

Faith. You know what I mean, all carnal and fleshly content.

Chr. Thank God you have escaped her: The abhorred of the Lord shall fall into her Ditch. a Pro. 22. 14

Faith. Nay, I know not whether I did wholly escape her, or no.

Chr. Why, I tro you did not consent to her desires?

Faith. No, not to defile my self;

Prov. 5. 4.
Job 31. 1.
for I remembred an old writing that
I had seen, which saith, *Her steps
take hold of Hell.* So I shut mine
eyes, because I would not be bewitch-
ed with her looks: then she railed
on me, and I went my way.

Chr. *Did you meet with no other af-
fault as you came ?*

He is af-
faulted by
Adam the
first.
Faith. When I came to the foot
of the Hill called *Difficulty* , I met
with a very aged Man, who asked
me, *What I was, and whither bound?*
I told him, That I was a Pilgrim, going to the Cœlestial City: Then said
the Old Man, *Thou lookest like an honest fellow; Wilt thou be content to
dwell with me, for the wages that I shall
give thee?* Then I asked him his name,
and where he dwelt? He said his
name was *Adam the first, and do dwell*
b Eph. 4.
22.
in the Town of Deceit. I asked him
then, What was his work? and what
the wages that he would give? He
told me, That his work was *many delights; and his wages, that I should be
his Heir at last.* I further asked him,
What House he kept, and what o-
ther Servants he had? so he told me,
*That his House was maintained with all
the dainties in the world, and that his*
Ser-

... came to my felf again, I cried ... mercy; but he faid, I know not ... how mercy, and with that knockt ... down again. He had doubtlefs ... a hand of me, but that one came by, and bid him forbear.

Chr. *Who was that, that bid him forbear?*

Faith. I did not know him at firft, but as he went by, I perceived the holes in his hands, and his fide; then I concluded that he was our Lord. So I went up the Hill.

Chr. *That Man that overtook you,* *was Mofes,* e *he fpareth none, neither knoweth he how to fhew mercy to thofe that tranfgrefs his Law.*

e The temper of Mofes.

Faith. I know it very well, it was not the firft time that he has met with me. 'Twas he that came to me when I dwelt fecurely at home, and that told me, He would burn my Houfe over my head, if I ftaid there.

Chr. *But did not you fee the Houfe that ftood there on the top of that Hill, on the fide of which* Mofes *met you?*

Faith. Yes, and the Lions too, before I came at it; but for the Lions, I think they were a fleep, for it was about Noon; and becaufe I had fo

much

much of the day before me, I paſſed by the Porter, and came down the Hill.

Chr. He told me indeed that he ſaw you go by, but I wiſh you had called at the Houſe; for. they would have ſhewed you ſo many Rarities, that you would ſcarce have forgot them to the day of your death. But pray tell me, did you meet no body in the Valley of Humility?

Faithfull aſſaulted by Diſcontent.

Faith. Yes, I met with one *Diſcontent*, who would willingly have perſwaded me to go back again with him: his reaſon was, for that the Valley was altogether without *Honour*; he told me moreover, That there to go, was the way to diſobey all my Friends, as Pride, Arogancy, Self-Conceit, worldly Glory, with others, who he knew, as he ſaid, would be very much offended, if I made ſuch a Fool of my ſelf, as to wade through this Valley.

Chr. Well, and how did you anſwer

Faithfuls anſwer to Diſcontent.

him?

Faith. I told him, That although all theſe that he named might claim kindred of me, and that rightly, (for indeed they were my Relations, *according to the fleſh*) yet ſince I became

a

again, they have disowned me, and I also have rejected them; and therefore they were to me now, no more then if they had never been of my Linage; I told him moreover, That as to this Valley, he had quite miss-reprefented the thing: *for before Honour is Humility, and a haughty spirit before a fall.* Therefore said I, I had rather go through this Valley to the Honour that was so accounted by the wifeft, then chufe that which he efteemed moft worth our affections.

Chr. *Met you with nothing elfe in that Valley?*

Faith. Yes, I met with *Shame*; But of all the Men that I met with in my Pilgrimage, he I think bears the wrong name: the other would be faid nay, after after a little argumentation, (and fome what elfe) but this bold faced *Shame*, would never have done.

He is affaulted with Shame.

Chr. *Why, what did he fay to you?*

Faith. What! why he objected againft Religion it felf; he faid it was a pitiful low fneaking bufinefs for a Man to mind Religion; he faid that a tender confcience was an un-manly thing, and that for a Man to watch
over

over his words and ways, so as to
tye up himself from that hectoring
liberty, that the brave spirits of the
times accustom themselves unto,
1 Cor. 1 would make me the Ridicule of the
26. ch. 3. times. He objected also, that but few
18. of the Mighty, Rich, or Wise, were
ever of my opinion; nor any of them,
Phil. 3. 7, 8. before they were perswaded to be
Fools, and to be of a voluntary fond-
ness, to venture the loss of all, *for
no body else knows what.* He moreover objected the base and low
estate and condition of those that
were chiefly the Pilgrims of the
times; in which they lived, also their
ignorance, and want of understanding in all natural Science. Yea, he
did hold me to it at that rate also, a-
bout a great many more things then
here I relate; as, that it was a *shame*
to sit whining and mourning under a
Sermon, and a *shame* to come sigh-
ing and groaning home. That it was
a shame to ask my Neighbour forgiveness for petty faults, or to make
restitution where I had taken from
any: he said also that Religion made
a man grow strange to the great, because of a few vices (which he called

(by finer names) and made him own and respect the base, because of the same Religious fraternity. And is not this, said he, a *shame*?

Chr. And what did you say to him?

Faith. Say! I could not tell what to say at the first. Yea, he put me so to it, that my blood came up in my face, even this *Shame* fetch't it up, and had almost beat me quite off. But at last I began to consider, *That that which is highly esteemed among Men, is bad in abomination with God.* And I thought again, This *Shame* tells me what men are, but it tells me nothing what God, or the word of God is. And I thought moreover, That at the day of doom we shall not be doomed to death or life, according to the hectoring spirits of the world; but according to the Wisdom and Law of the Highest. Therefore thought I, what God says, is best, is best, though all the Men in the world are against it. Seeing then, that God prefers his Religion, seeing God prefers a tender Conscience, seeing they that make themselves Fools for the Kingdom of Heaven, are wisest; and that the

poor

poor that loveth Chrift, is richer then
the greateſt Man in the world that
hates him; *Shame* depart, thou art
an Enemy to my Salvation: ſhall I
entertain thee againſt my Soveraign
Lord? How then ſhall I look him in
the face at his coming? Should I
now be *aſhamed* of his ways and Servants, how can I expeſt the bleſſing? But indeed this *Shame* was a
bold Villain; I could ſcarce ſhake him
out of my company; yea, he would
be haunting of me, and continually
whiſpering me in the ear, with ſome
one or other of the infirmities that
attend Religion: but at laſt I told
him, 'Twas but in vain to attempt further in this buſineſs; for thoſe things
that he diſdained, in thoſe did I ſee
moſt glory: And ſo at laſt I got paſt
this *importunate* one.

Mar. 8. 38.

The tryals that thoſe men do meet withal
That are obedient to the Heavenly call,
Are manifold, and ſuited to the fleſh,
And come, and come, and come again
  afreſh;
That now, or ſomtime elſe, we by them
  may
Be taken, overcome, and caſt away.

O

Or let the Pilgrims, let the Pilgrims
  then,
Be vigilant, and quit themselves like
  men.

Chr. *I am glad, my Brother, that
thou didst withstand this Villain so
bravely; for of all, as thou sayst, I think
he has the wrong name: for he is so bold
as to follow us in the Streets, and to attempt to put us to shame before all men;
that is, to make us ashamed of that
which is good: but if he was not himself
audacious, he would never attempt to do
as he does, but let us still resist him: for
notwithstanding all his Bravadoes, he
promoteth the Fool, and none else.* The
Wise shall Inherit Glory, *said* Solo-
mon, but shame shall be the promo- Prov.3.35.
tion of Fools.

Faith. *I think we must cry to him for
help against shame, that would have us
be valiant for the Truth upon the Earth.*

Chr. *You say true. But did you meet
no body else in that Valley ?*

Faith. No, not I, for I had Sun-shine
all the rest of the way, through that,
and also through the Valley of the
shadow of death.

Chr.

Chr. 'Twas well for you, I am sure it fared far otherwise with me. I had for a long season, as soon almost as I entred into that Valley, a dreadful Combat with that foul Fiend *Apollyon :* Yea, I thought verily he would have killed me; especially when he got me down, and crusht me under him, as if he would have crusht me to pieces. For as he threw me, my Sword flew out of my hand; nay he told me, *He was sure of me :* but *I cried to God, and he heard me, and delivered me out of all my troubles.* Then I entred into the Valley of the shadow of death, and had no light for almost half the way through it. I thought I should a been killed there, over, and over ; But at last, day brake, and the Sun rise, and I went through that which was behind with far more ease and quiet

Moreover, I saw in my Dream, that as they went on, *Faithful,* as he chanced to look on one side, saw a Man whose name is *Talkative,* walking at a distance besides them, (for .n this place, there was room enough

Talkative for them all to walk) *He was a tall*
described. *Man, and somthing more comely at a*
distance

distance then at hand. To this Man *Faithful* addreſſed himſelf in this manner.

Faith. *Friend, Whither away? Are you going to the Heavenly Countrey?*

Talk. I am going to that ſame place.

Faith. *That is well: Then I hope we may have your good Company.*

Talk. With a very good will, will I be your Companion.

Faith. *Come on then, and let us go together, and let us ſpend our time in diſcourſing of things that are profitable.* Faithful andTalka-tive enter diſcourſe.

Talk. To talk of things that are good, to me is very acceptable, with you, or with any other ; and I am glad that I have met with thoſe that incline to ſo good a work. For to ſpeak the truth, there are but few that care thus to ſpend their time (as they are in their travels) but chuſe much rather to be ſpeaking of things to no profit, and this hath been a trouble to me. Talkative diſlike of bad diſ-courſe.

Faith. *That is indeed a thing to be lamented; for what things ſo worthy of the uſe of the tongue and mouth of men on Earth, as are the things of the God of Heaven?*

H   *Talk.*

Talk. I like you wonderful well, for your saying is full of conviction; and I will add, What thing so pleasant, and what so profitable, as to talk of the things of God?

What things so pleasant? (that is, if a man hath any delight in things that are wonderful) for instance: If a man doth delight to talk of the History or the Mystery of things, or if a man doth love to talk of Miracles, Wonders or Signs, where shall he find things Recorded so delightful, and so sweetly penned, as in the holy Scripture?

Faith. That's true: but to be profited by such things in our talk, should be that which we design.

Talk. That it is that I said: for to *talk* of such things is most profitable, for by so doing, a Man may get knowledge of many things, as of the vanity of earthly things, and the benefit of things above: (thus in general) but more particularly, By this a man may learn the necessity of the Newbirth, the insufficiency of our works, the need of Christs righteousness, &c. Besides, by this a man may learn by *talk,* what it is to repent, to believe,

Talkatives fine-discourse.

to

... or the like: By this
... may learn what are the
... promises & consolations of the
... to his own comfort. Further,
... this a Man may learn to refute
... opinions, to vindicate the truth,
and also to instruct the ignorant.

Faith. *All this is true, and glad am I to hear these things from you.*

Talk. Alas! the want of this is the cause that so few understand the need of faith, and the necessity of a work of Grace in their Soul, in order to eternal life: but ignorantly live in the works of the Law, by which a man can by no means obtain the Kingdom of Heaven.

Faith. *But by your leave, Heavenly knowledge of these, is the gift of God; no man attaineth to them by humane industry, or only by the talk of them.*

Talk. All this I know very well, for a man can receive nothing except it be given him from Heaven; all is of Grace, not of works: I could give you an hundred Scriptures for the confirmation of this.

O brave Talkative

Faith. *Well then, said Faithful, what is that one thing, that we shall at this time found our discourse upon?*

H 2 Talk.

O brave Talkative.

Talk. What you will: I will talk of things Heavenly, or things Earthly; things Moral, or things Evangelical; things Sacred, or things Prophanes; things paſt, or things to come; things forraign, or things at home; things more Eſſential, or things Circum-ſtantial: provided that all be done to our profit.

Faith. Now did *Faithful* begin to wonder; *and ſtepping to* Chriſtian, *(for*

Faithful beguiled by Talkative. *he walked all this while by himſelf,) he ſaid to him, (but ſoftly) What a brave Companion have we got! Surely this man will make a very excellent Pilgrim.*

Chriſtian makes a diſcovery of Talkative, telling Faithful who he was.

Chr: At this *Chriſtian* modeſtly ſmiled, and ſaid, This man with whom you are ſo taken, will beguile with this tongue of his, twenty of them that know him not.

Faith: *Do you know him then?*

Chr. Know him! Yes, better then he knows himſelf.

Faith. *Pray what is he?*

Chr. His name is *Talkative*, he dwelleth in our Town; I wonder that you ſhould be a ſtranger to him, only I conſider that our Town is large.

Faith.

*Faith. Whose Son is he? And where-
about doth he dwell?*

Chr. He is the Son of one *Saywell*,
he dwelt in *Prating-row*; and he is
known of all that are acquainted
with him, by the name of *Talkative*
in *Prating-row*: and notwithstanding his fine tongue, he is but a sorry
fellow.

Faith. *Well, he seems to be a very
pretty man.*

Chr. That is, to them that have
not through acquaintance with him,
for he is best abroad, near home he is
ugly enough: your saying, That he
is a *pretty man*, brings to my mind
what I have observed in the work of
the Painter, whose Pictures shews
best at a distance; but very near,
more unpleasing.

Faith. *But I am ready to think you
do but* jest, *because you* smiled.

Chr. God-forbid that I should *jest*,
(though I smiled) in this matter, or
that I should accuse any falsely; I
will give you a further discovery of
him: This man is for any company,
and for any *talk*; as he *talketh now*
with you, so will he *talk* when he is
on the *Ale-bench*: and the more

H 3   drink

drink he hath in his crown, the more of these things he hath in his mouth: Religion hath no place in his heart, or house, or conversation; all he hath, lieth in his *tongue*, and his Religion is to make a noise *therewith*.

Faith. Say you so! Then I am in this man greatly deceived.

Chr. Deceived! you may be sure of it. Remember the Proverb, *They say and do not: but the Kingdom of God is not in word, but in power.* He

talketh of Prayer, of Repentance, of Faith, and of the New birth: but he knows but only to *talk* of them. I have been in his Family, and have observed him both at home and a-

broad; and I know what I say of him is the truth. His house is as empty of Religion, *as the white of an Egg is of savour.* There is there, neither Prayer, nor sign of Repentance for sin: Yea, the bruit in his kind serves God far better then he. He is the very stain, reproach, and shame of

Religion to all that know him; it can hardly have a good word in all that end of the Town where he dwells, through him. Thus say the common
People

People that know him, *A Saint a- broad, and a* Devil *at home*: His poor Family finds it so, he is such a *churl*, such a railer at, and so unreasonable with his Servants, that they neither know how to do for, or speak to him. Men that have any dealings with him, say 'tis better to deal with a Turk then with him, for fairer deal- ing they shall have at their hands. This *Talkative*, if it be possible, will go beyond them, defraud, beguile, and over-reach them. Besides, he brings up his Sons to follow his steps; and if he findeth in any of them *a foolish timorousnes* (for so he calls the first appearance of a tender con- science) he calls them fools and block- heads; and by no means will imploy them in much, or speak to their commendations before others. For my part I am of opinion, that he has by his wicked life caused many to stumble and fall; and will be, if God prevent not, the ruine of many more.

Faith. *Well, my Brother, I am bound to believe you; not only because you say you know him, but also because like a Christian you make your reports*

H 4   of

of men. For I cannot think that you speak these things of ill will, but because it is even so as you say.

Chr. Had I known him no more than you, I might perhaps have thought of him as at the first you did: Yea, had he received this report at *their* hands only that are enemies to Religion, I should have thought it had been a slander: (A Lot that often falls from bad mens mouths upon good mens Names and Professions:) But all these things, yea and a great many more as bad, of my own knowledge I can prove him guilty of. Besides, good men are ashamed of him, they can neither call him *Brother* nor *Friend*; the very naming of him among them, makes them blush, if they know him.

Fa. Well, I see that Saying and Doing are two things, and hereafter I shall better observe this distinction.

Chr. They are *two* things indeed, and are as diverse as are the Soul and the Body: For as the Body without the Soul, is but a dead Carkass; so, *Saying*, if it be alone, is but a dead Carkass also. The Soul of Religion is the practick part: *Pure Reli-*

The Carkass of Religion.

ion

gion and undefiled, before God and the
Father, is this, To visit the Fatherless
and Widows in their affliction, and to
keep himself unspoted from the World.
This *Talkative* is not aware of, he
thinks that *bearing* and *saying* will
make a good Chriftian, and thus he
deceiveth his own foul. Hearing is
but as the fowing of the Seed; talking is not fufficient to prove that
fruit is indeed in the heart and life;
and let us affure our felves, that at
the day of Doom, men fhall be judged according to their fruits. It will
not be faid then, *Did you believe?* but,
were you *Doers*, or *Talkers* only? and
accordingly fhall they be judged. The
end of the World is compared to our
Harveft, and you know men at
Harveft regard nothing but Fruit.
Not that any thing can be accepted
that is not of Faith : But I fpeak this,
to fhew you how infignificant the
profeffion of *Talkative* will be at that
day.

Fa. *This brings to my mind that of*
Mofes, *by which he defcribeth the beaft*
that is clean. *He is fuch an one that*
parteth the Hoof, and cheweth the Cud:
Not that parteth the Hoof only, or that
                                 cheweth

Marginal notes:
James 1. 27. fee ver. 22, 23, 24, 25, 26.

See Mat. 13. and ch. 25.

Levit. 11. Deut. 14.

Faithful convinced of the badness of Talkative. cheweth the Cud only. The Hare cheweth the Cud, but yet is unclean, because he parteth not the Hoof. And this truly resembleth Talkative; he cheweth the Cud, he seeketh knowledge, he cheweth upon the Word, but he divideth not the Hoof, he parteth not with the way of sinners; but as the Hare, retaineth the foot of a Dog, or Bear, and therefore he is unclean.

Chr. You have spoken, for ought I know, the true Gospel sense of those Texts, and I will add an other thing. 1. Cor. 13. 1, 2, 3. ch. 14. 7. *Paul* calleth some men, yea and those great Talkers too, sounding Brass, and Tinckling Cymbals; that Talkative like to things that sound without life. is, as he Expounds them in another place, *Things without life, giving sound.* Things without life, that is, without the true Faith and Grace of the Gospel; and consequently, things that shall never be placed in the Kingdom of Heaven among those that are the Children of life: Though their *sound* by their *talk*, be as if it were the *Tongue* or voice of an Angel.

Fait. Well, I was not so fond of his company at first, but I am sick of it now. What shall we do to be rid of him?

Chr.

Chr. Take my advice, and do as I bid you, and you shall find that he will soon be sick of your Company too, except God shall touch his heart and turn it.

Fait. What would you have me to do?

Chr. Why, go to him, and enter into some serious discourse about *the power of Religion*: And ask him plainly (when he has approved of it, for that he will) whether this thing be set up in his Heart, House or Conversation.

Fait. Then *Faithful* stept forward again, and said to *Talkative*: *Come, what chear? how is it now?*

Talk. Thank you, Well. I thought we should have had a great deal of *Talk* by this time.

Fait. Well, if you will, we will fall to it now; and since you left it with me to state the question, let be this: How doth the saving grace of God discover it self, when it is in the heart of man?

Talk. I perceive then that our talk must be *about the power of things*; Well, 'tis a very good question, and I shall be willing to answer you. And take my answer in brief thus. First, *Where the Grace of God is in the heart,*

Talkatives false discovery of a work of grace

it

it causeth there *a great out-cry against sin.* Secondly ———

Fait. *Nay hold, let us consider of one at once: I think you should rather say, It shows it self by inclining the Soul to abhor its sin.*

Talk. Why, what difference is there between crying out against, and abhoring of sin?

Fait. *Oh! a great deal; a man may*

cry out against sin, of policy; but he cannot abhor it, but by vertue of a Godly antipathy against it: I have heard many cry out against sin in the Pulpit, who yet can abide it well enough in the heart, and house, and conversation. Josephs Mistris cried out with aloud voice, as if she had been very holy; but she would willingly, notwithstanding that, have committed uncleanness with him. Some cry out against sin, even as the Mother cries out against her Child in her lap, when she calleth it Slut and naughty Girl, and then falls to hugging and kissing it.

Talk. You lie at the catch, I perceive.

Fait. *No, not I, I am only for seting things right. But what is the second thing whereby you would prove a discovery*

covery of a work of grace in the heart?

Talk. Great knowledge of Gospel Myſteries.

Fait. This ſigne ſhould have been firſt, but firſt or laſt, it is alſo falſe; for, Knowledge, great knowledge, may be obtained in the myſteries of the Goſpel, and yet no work of grace in the Soul. Yea, if a man have all knowledge, he may yet be nothing, and ſo conſequently be no child of God. When Chriſt ſaid, Do you know all theſe things? And the Diſciples had anſwered, Yes: He addeth, Bleſſed are ye if ye do them. He doth not lay the bleſſing in the knowing of them, but in the doing of them. For there is a knowledge that is not attained with doing: He that knoweth his Maſters will, and doth it not. A man may know like an Angel, and yet be no Chriſtian; therefore your ſign is not true. Indeed to know, is a thing that pleaſeth Talkers and Boaſters; but to do, is that which pleaſeth God. Not that the heart can be good without knowledge, for without that the heart is naught: There is therefore knowledge, and knowledge. Knowledge that reſteth in the bare ſpeculation of things, and knowledge that is accompanied with the grace of faith and love, which puts a

man

Great knowledge no ſign of grace

1 Cor. 13.

Knowledge and knowledge.

man upon doing even the will of God
from the heart: the first of these will
serve the Talker, but without the other
the true Christian is not content. Give
me underſtanding, and I ſhall keep thy

True know-
ledge at-
tended
with en-
deavours.
Law, yea I ſhall obſerve it with my
whole heart, Pſal. 119. 34.

Talk. You lie at the catch again,
this is not for edification.

Fait. *Well, if you pleaſe propound*
another ſign how this work of grace diſ-
covereth it ſelf where it is.

Talk. Not I, for I ſee we ſhall not
agree.

Fait. *Well, if you will not, will you*
give me leave to do it?

Talk. You may uſe your Liberty.

Fait. *A work of grace in the ſoul diſ-*

One good
ſigne ſgrace
Joh. 16. 8.
Rom. 7. 24.
Joh. 16. 9.
Mar. 16, 16
Pſ. 38. 18.
Jer. 31. 19.
Gal. 2. 15.
Act 4. 12.
Mat. 5. 6.
Rev. 21. 6.
covereth it ſelf, either to him that hath
it, or to ſtanders by.

To him that hath it, thus. *It gives*
him conviction of ſin, eſpecially of the
defilement of his nature, and the ſin of
unbelief, (for the ſake of which he is
ſure to be damned, if he findeth not
mercy at Gods hand by faith in Jeſus
Chriſt.) This ſight and ſenſe of things
worketh in him ſorrow and ſhame for ſin;
he findeth moreover revealed in him
the Saviour of the World, and the ab-
ſolute

...late necessity of closing with him for life, at the which he findeth hungrings and thirstings after him, to which hungrings, &c. the promise is made. Now according to the strength or weakness of his Faith in his Saviour, so is his joy and peace, so is his love to holiness, so are his desires to know him more, and also to serve him in this World. But though I say it discovereth it self thus unto him; yet it is but seldom that he is able to conclude that this is a work of Grace, because his corruptions now, and his abused reason, makes his mind to mis-judge in this matter; therefore in him that hath this work, there is required a very sound Judgement, before he can with steddiness conclude that this is a work of Grace.

To others it is thus discovered.

1. By an experimental confession of his Faith in Christ. 2. By a life answerable to that confession, to wit, a life of holiness; heart-holiness, family-holiness, (if he hath a Family) and by Conversation-holiness in the world: which in the general teacheth him, inwardly to abhor his Sin, and himself for that in secret, to suppress it in his Family, and to promote holiness in the World;

Ro. 10. 10.
Phi. 1. 27.
Mat. 5. 9.
Jo. 24. 15.
Pl. 50. 23.
Job. 42.
5, 6.
Ezek. 29.
43

not

not by talk only, as an Hypocrite or Talkative Person may do: but by a practical Subjection in Faith, and Love, to the power of the word: And now Sir, as to this brief description of the work of Grace, and also the discovery of it, if you have ought to object, object: if not, then give me leave to propound to you a second question.

Another good sign of Grace. Talk. Nay, my part is not now to object, but to hear, let me therefore have your second question.

Faith. It is this, Do you experience the first part of this description of it? and doth your life and conversation testifie the same? or standeth your Religion in Word or in Tongue, and not in Deed and Truth? pray, if you incline to answer me in this, say no more then you know the God above will say Amen to; and also, nothing but what your Conscience can justifie you in. For, not he that commendeth himself is approved, but whom the Lord commendeth. Besides, to say I am thus, and thus, when my Conversation, and all *Talkative not pleased with* my Neighbours tell me, I lye, is great wickedness.

Faithfuls question. Talk. Then Talkative at first began to blush, but recovering himself,

Thus

Thus he replyed, You come now to Experience, to Conscience, and God: and to appeals to him for justification of what is spoken: This kind of discourse I did not expect, nor am I disposed to give an answer to such questions, because I count not my self bound thereto, unless you take upon you to be a *Catechizer*; and, though you should so do, yet I may refuse to make you my Judge: But I pray will you tell me, why you ask me such questions?

Faith. *Because I saw you forward to talk, and because I knew not that you had ought else but notion. Besides to tell you all the Truth, I have heard of you, that you are a Man whose Religion lies in talk, and that your Conversation gives this your Mouth-profession, the lye. They say You are a spot among Christians, and that Religion fareth the worse for your ungodly conversation, that some already have stumbled at your wicked ways, and that more are in danger of being destroyed thereby; your Religion, and an Ale-House, and Covetousness, and uncleanness, and swearing, and lying, and vain Company-keeping, &c. will stand together.*

I

gether. The proverb is true of you, which is said of a Whore; to wit That she is a shame to all Women; so you are ashame to all Professors.

Talk. Since you are ready to take up reports, and to judge so rashly as you do; I cannot but conclude you are some peevish, or melancholly Man, not fit to be discoursed with, and so adieu.

Chr. Then came up *Christian*, and said to his Brother, I told you how it would happen, your words and his lusts could not agree; he had rather leave your company, then reform his life: but he is gone as I said, let him go; the loss is no mans but his own, he has saved us the trouble of going from him; for he continuing, as I suppose he will do, as he is, he would have been but a blot in our Company: besides, the Apostle says, *From such withdraw thy self.*

Faith. *But I am glad we had this little discourse with him, it may happen that he will think of it again; however, I have dealt plainly with him, and so am clear of his blood, if he perisheth.*

Chr. You did well to talk so plainly

[margin notes]
Talkative flings away from Faithful.

A good riddance.

ly to him as you did, there is but little of this faithful dealing with men now a days; and that makes Religion so stink in the nostrills of many, as it doth: for they are these *Talkative* Fools, whose Religion is only in word, and are debauched and vain in their Conversation, that (being so much admitted into the Fellowship of the Godly) do stumble the World, blemish Christianity, and grieve the Sincere. I wish that all Men would deal with such, as you have done, then should they either be made more conformable to Religion, or the company of Saints would be too hot for them.

How Talkative *at first lifts up his Plumes!*

How bravely doth he speak! how he presumes

To drive down all before him! but so soon

As Faithful *talks of* Heart work, *like the Moon*

That's past the full, into the wain he goes;

And so will all, but he that Heart work *knows.*

Thus

Thus they went on talking of what they had seen by the way; and so made that way easie, which would otherwise, no doubt, have been tedious to them: for now they went through a Wilderness.

Then I saw in my Dream, that when they were got out of the Wilderness, they presently saw a Town before them, and the name of that Town is *Vanity*; and at the Town there is a *Fair* kept, called *Vanity-Fair*: It is kept all the Year long, it beareth the name of *Vanity-Fair*, because the Town where tis kept, *is lighter then* Vanity; and also, because all that is there sold, or that cometh thither, is *Vanity*. As is the saying of the wise, *All that cometh is vanity*.

Isa. 40. 17
Eccl. 1.
chap. 2. 11
17.

This Fair is no new erected business, but a thing of Ancient standing; I will shew you the original of it.

The Antiquity of this Fair.

Almost five thousand years agone, there were Pilgrims walking to the Cœlestial City, as these two honest persons are; and *Beelzebub*, *Apollyon*, and *Legion*, with their Companions, perceiving by the path that the Pilgrims made, that their way to the City lay through *this Town*

Town of Vanity, they contrived here to set up a Fair; a Fair wherein should be sold of *all sorts of Vanity*, and that it should last all the year long. Therefore at *this Fair* are all such Merchandize sold, As Houses, Lands, Trades, Places, Honours, Preferments, Titles, Countreys, Kingdoms, Lusts, Pleasures and Delights of all sorts, as Whores, Bauds, Wives, Husbands, Children, Masters, Servants, Lives, Blood, Bodies, Souls, Silver, Gold, Pearls, precious Stones, and what not.

The Merchandize of this Fair.

And moreover, at this Fair there is at all times to be seen Juglings, Cheats, Games, Plays, Fools, Apes, Knaves, and Rogues, and that of all sorts.

Here are to be seen, and that for nothing, Thefts, Murders, Adultries, False-swearers, and that of a blood-red colour.

And as in others fairs of less moment, there are the several Rows and Streets, under their proper names, where such and such Wares are vended: So here likewise, you have the proper Places, Rows, Streets, (*viz.* Countreys and Kingdoms,) where the Wares of this Fair are

I 3   soonest

The Street of this fair. sooneft to be found: Here is the _Britain_ Row, the _French_ Row, the _Italian_ Row, the _Spanish_ Row, the _German_ Row, where feveral forts of Vanities are to be fold. But as in other _fairs_ fome one Commodity is as the chief of all the _fair_, fo the Ware of _Rome_ and her Merchandize is greatly promoted in _this fair_: Only our _English_ Nation, with fome others, have taken a diflike thereat.

1 Cor. 5 10.
Chrift went through this fair Now, as I faid, the way to the Cœleftial City lyes juft thorow _this Town_, where this lufty Fair is kept; and he that will go to the City, and yet not go thorow this Town, _muft needs go out of the World._ The Prince of Princes himfelf, when here, went through _this Town_ to his own Countrey, and that upon a _Fair-day too_:
Mat. 4. 8.
Luke 4, 5.
6, 7. Yea, and as I think, it was _Beelzebub_ the chief Lord of this _Fair_, that invited him to buy of his _Vanities_; yea, would have made him Lord of the _Fair_, would he but have done him Reverence as he went thorow the _Town_. Yea, becaufe he was fuch a perfon of Honour, _Beelzebub_ had him from _Street_ to _Street_, and fhewed him all the Kingdoms of
the

the World in a little time, that he might, if possible, alure that Blessed One, to *cheapen* and *buy* some of his Vanities. But he had no mind to the Merchandize, and therefore left the Town, without laying out so much as one Farthing upon these *Vanities*. This *Fair* therefore is an Ancient thing, of long standing, and a very great *Fair*.

Christ bought nothing in this fair

Now these Pilgrims, as I said, must needs go thorow this *fair*: Well, so they did; but behold, even as they entred into the *fair*, all the people in the *fair* were moved, and the Town it self as it were in a Hubbub about them; and that for several reasons: For,

The Pilgrims enter the fair

The fair in a hubbub about them.

First, The Pilgrims were cloathed with such kind of Raiment, as was diverse from the Raiment of any that Traded in that *fair*. The people therefore of the *fair* made a great gazing upon them: Some said they were Fools, some they were Bedlams, and some they are Outlandish-men.

The first cause of the hubbub.

Secondly, And as they wondred at their Apparel, so they did likewise at their Speech, for few could understand what they said; they naturally spoke the Language of *Canaan*

1 *Cor.* 2. 7, 8. *2d. Cause of the hubbub.*

but

but they that kept the *fair*, were the men of this World: So that from one end of the *fair* to the other, they seemed *Barbarians* each to the other.

Thirdly, But that which did not a little amuse the Merchandizers, was, that these Pilgrims set very light by all their Wares, they cared not, so much as to look upon them: and if they called upon them to buy, they would put their fingers in their ears, and cry, *Turn away mine eyes from beholding vanity*; and look upwards, signifying that their Trade and Traffick was in Heaven.

One chanced mockingly, beholding the carriages of the men, to say unto them, What will ye buy? but they, looking gravely upon him, said, *We buy the Truth*. At that, there was an occasion taken to despise the men the more; some mocking, some taunting, some speaking reproachfully, and some calling upon others to smite them. At last things came to an hubbub and great stir in the *fair*, in so much that all order was confounded. Now was word presently brought to the *great one* of the *fair*, who quickly came down, and deputed some of his

Phil. 119. 37.

Phil. 3. 19 20.

Pf. 23. 23.

They are mocked.

The fair in a hubbub.

his most trusty friends to take these
men into examination, about whom *They are*
the *fair* was almost overturned. So *examined.*
the men were brought to examina-
tion; and they that sat upon them,
asked them whence they came, whether they went, and what they did
there in such an unusual Garb? The *They tell*
men told them, that they were Pil- *who they*
grims and Strangers in the World, *are and*
and that they were going to their *whence*
own Countrey, which was the Hea- *they came.*
venly *Jerusalem*; and that they had
given none occasion to the men of the
Town, nor yet to the Merchandizers, thus to abuse them, and to let
them in their Journey. Except it was,
for that, when one asked them what
they would buy, they said they would
buy the Truth. But they that were *They are*
appointed to examine them, did not *not believ-*
believe them to be any other then *ed.*
Bedlams and Mad, or else such as
came to put all things into a confusion
in the *fair*. Therefore they took them *They are*
and beat them, and besmeared them *put in the*
with dirt, and then put them into *Cage.*
theCage, that they might be made
a Spectacle to all the men of the *fair*.
There therefore they lay for some
                                    time,

time, and were made the objects of
any mans sport, or malice, or re-
venge. The great one of the *fair*
laughing still at all that befel them.
But the men being patient, and not
rendering railing for railing, but con-
trarywise blessing, and giving good
words for bad, and kindness for in-
juries done: Some men in the *fair*
that were more observing, and less
prejudiced then the rest, began to
check and blame the baser sort for
their continual abuses done by them
to the men: They therefore in angry
manner let fly at them again, count-
ing them as bad as the men in the
Cage, and telling them that they
seemed confederates, and should be
made partakers of their misfortunes.
The other replied, That for ought
they could see, the men were quiet,
and sober, and intended no body any
harm; and that there were many
that Traded in their *fair*, that were
more worthy to be put into the Cage,
yea, and Pillory too, then were the
men that they had abused. Thus,
after divers words had passed on both
sides, (the men themselves behaving
themselves all the while very wisely
and

*Their be-
haviour in
the Cage.*

*The men of
the fair do
fall out a-
mong them-
selves a-
bout these
two men.*

and soberly before them,) they fell
to some Blows, and did harm one to
another. Then were these two poor *They are*
men brought before their Examiners *made the Authors of*
again, and there charged as being *this distur-*
guilty of the late Hubbub that had *bance.*
been in the *fair*. So they beat them *They are*
pitifully, and hanged Irons upon *led up and*
them, and led them in Chaines, up *down the*
and down the *fair*, for an example *fair in*
and a terror to others, left any should *Chaines for*
further speak in their behalf, or joyn *others.*
themselves unto them. But *Christian*
and *Faithful* behaved themselves yet
more wisely, and received the igno-
miny and shame that was cast upon
them, with so much meeknefs and
patience, that it won to their side *Some of the*
(though but few in comparison of the *men of the*
rest) several of the men in the *fair*. This *fair won to*
put the other party yet into a greater *them.*
rage, insomuch that they concluded
the death of these two men. Where- *Their ad-*
fore they threatned that the Cage nor *versaries*
Irons should serve their turn, but that *resolve to*
they should die, for the abuse they *kill them.*
had done, and for deluding the men
of the *fair*.

Then were they remanded to the
Cage again until further order should
be

taken with them. So they put them in, and made their feet faft in the Stocks. Then a convenient time being appointed, they brought them forth to their Tryal in order to their Condemnation. When the time was come, they were brought before their Enemies and arraigned; the Judge's name was Lord *Hategood.* Their Indictment was one and the fame in fubftance, though fomewhat varying in form; the Contents whereof was this.

They are again put into the Cage and after brought to Tryal.

That they were enemies to, an l difturbers of their Trade; that they had made Commotions and Divifions in the Town, and had won a party to their own moft dangerous opinions, in contempt of the Law of their Prince.

Their Indictment.

Then *Faithful* began to anfwer, That he had only fet himfelf againft that which had fet it felf againft him that is higher then the higheft. And faid he, As for difturbance, I make none, being my felf a man of Peace; the Party that were won to us, were won by beholding our Truth and Innocence, and they are only turned from the worfe to the better. And as to the King you talk of, fince he is

Faithfuls anfwer for himfelf.

Beelzebub

Beelzebub, the Enemy of our Lord,
I defie him and all his Angels.

Then Proclamation was made, that
they that had ought to say for their
Lord the King against the Prisoner at
the Bar, should forthwith appear and
give in their evidence. So there came
in three Witnesses, to wit, *Envy*, *Su-*
perstition, and *Pickthank*. They was
then asked, If they knew the Prisoner at the Bar? and what they had
to say for their Lord the King against
him.

Then stood forth *Envy*, and said to
this effect; My Lord, I have known
this man a long time, and will attest
upon my Oath before this honourable Bench, That he is——

Judge. Hold, give him his Oath;
So they sware him. Then he said, My
Lord, This man, notwithstanding his
plausible name, is one of the vilest
men in our Countrey; He neither
regardeth Prince nor People, Law
nor Custom: but doth all that he can
to possess all men with certain of his
disloyal notions, which he in the
general calls Principles of Faith and
Holiness. And in particular, I heard
him once my self affirm, *That Chri-*
stianity

stianity, and the Customs of our Town of Vanity, were Diametrically opposite, and could not be reconciled. By which saying, my Lord, he doth at once, not only condemn all our laudable doings, but us in the doing of them.

Judg. Then did the Judge say to him, Haft thou any more to say?

Env. My Lord I could say much more, only I would not be tedious to the Court. Yet if need be, when the other Gentlemen have given in their Evidence, rather then any thing fhall be wanting that will difpatch him, I will enlarge my Teftimony againft him. So he was bid ftand by. Then they called *Superftition*, and bid him look upon the Prifoner; they alfo asked, What he could fay for their Lord the King againft him? Then they fware him, fo he began.

Super. My Lord, I have no great acquaintance with this man, nor do I defire to have further knowledge of him; However this I know, that he is a very peftilent fellow, from fome difcourfe that the other day I had with him in this *Town*; for then talking with him, I heard him fay,

That

That our Religion was naught, and
such by which a man could by no
means please God : which sayings of
his, my Lord, your Lordship very
well knows, what necessarily thence
will follow, *two wit*, That we still do
worship in vain, are yet in our Sins,
and finally shall be damned ; and
this is that which I have to say.

Then was *Pickthank* sworn, and
bid say what he knew, in behalf of
their Lord the King against the Prisoner at the Bar.

Pick. My Lord, and you Gentlemen all, This fellow I have known of
a long time, and have heard him
speak things that ought not to be
spoke. For he hath railed on our
noble Prince *Beelzebub*, and hath
spoke contemptibly of his honourable Friends, whose names are the Lord
Oldman, the Lord *Carnal delight*, the
Lord *Luxurious*, the Lord *Desire of
Vain-glory*, my old Lord *Lechery*, Sir
Having Greedy, with all the rest
of our Nobility ; and he hath said
moreover, that if all men were of
his mind, if possible, there is not
one of these noble Men should have
any longer a being in this Town.
Besides,

*Pick-
thank's
Testimony.*

*Sins are all
Lords and
Great ones.*

Besides, he hath not been afraid to rail on you, my Lord, who are now appointed to be his Judge, calling you an ungodly Villian, with many other such like vilifying terms, by which he hath befpattered moft of the Gentry of our Town. When this *Picktbank* had told his tale, the Judge directed his speech to the Prifoner at the Bar, faying, Thou Runa- *Faithful* gate, Heretick, and Traitor, haft *defence of* thou heard what thefe honeft Gentle- *himself.* men have witneffed againft thee?

Faith. *May I fpeak a few words in my own defence?*

Judg. Sirrah, Sirrah, thou deferveft to live no longer, but to be flain immediately upon the place; yet that all men may fee our gentlenefs towards thee, let us fee what thou haft to fay.

Faith. 1. I fay then in anfwer to what Mr. *Envy* hath fpoken, I never faid ought but this, *That what Rule, or Laws, or Cuftom, or People, were flat againft the Word of God, are diametrically oppofite to Chriftianity.* If I have faid a mifs in this, convince me of my errour, and I am ready here before you to make my recantation.

2. As

2. As to the second, to wit, Mr. *Superstition*, and his charge against me, I said only this, *That in the worship of God there is required a divine Faith; but there can be no divine Faith, without a divine Revelation of the will of God: therefore whatever is thrust into the worship of God, that is not agreeable to a divine Revelation, cannot be done but by an humane Faith, which Faith will not profit to Eternal life.*

3. As to what Mr. *Pickthank* hath said, I say, (avoiding terms, as that I am said to rail, and the like) That the Prince of this Town, with all the Rablement his Attendants, by this Gentlemen named, are more fit for a being in Hell, then in this Town and Countrey; *and so the Lord have mercy upon me.*

Then the Judge called to the Jury (who all this while stood by, to hear and observe) Gentlemen of the Jury, you see this man about whom so great an uproar hath been made in this Town: you have also heard what these worthy Gentlemen have witnessed against him; also you have heard his reply and confession: It lieth now in your brests to hang him,

The Judge his speech to the Jury.

K   or

or save his life. But yet I think meet to instruct you into our Law.

There was an Act made in the days

Exod. 1. of *Pharaoh* the Great, Servant to our Prince, That left those of a contrary Religion should multiply and grow too strong for him, their Males should be thrown into the River. There was also an Act made in the days of *Ne-*

Dan. 3. *buchadnezzar* the Great, another of his Servants, That whoever would not fall down and worship his golden Image, should be thrown into a fiery Furnace. There was also an

Dan. 6. Act made in the days of *Darius*, That who so, for some time, called upon any God but his, should be cast into the Lions Den. Now the substance of these Laws this Rebel has broken, not only in thought (which is not to be born) but also in word and deed; which must therefore needs be intollerable.

For that of *Pharaoh*, his Law was made upon a supposition, to prevent mischief, no Crime being yet apparent; but here is a Crime apparent. For the second and third, you see he disputeth against our Religion; and for the Treason he hath confessed, he deserveth to die the death. Then

Then went the Jury out, whose names were, Mr. *Blind-man*, Mr. *No-good*, Mr. *Malice*, Mr. *Love-luſt*, Mr. *Live-looſe*, Mr. *Heady*, Mr. *High-mind*, Mr. *Enmity*, Mr. *Lyar*, Mr. *Cruelty*, Mr. *Hate-light*, and Mr. *Implacable*, who every one gave in his private Verdict againſt him among themſelves, and afterwards unanimouſly concluded to bring him in guilty before the Judge. And firſt Mr. *Blind-man*, the foreman, ſaid, *I ſee clearly that this man is an Heretick*. Then ſaid Mr. *No-good*, *Away with ſuch a fellow from the Earth*. *Ay*, ſaid Mr. *Malice*, *for I hate the very looks of him*. Then ſaid Mr. *Love-luſt*, *I could never indure him*. *Nor I*, ſaid Mr. *Live-looſe*, *for he would alwayes be condemning my way*. *Hang him, hang him*, ſaid Mr. *Heady*. *A ſorry Scrub*, ſaid Mr. *High-mind*. *My heart riſeth againſt him*, ſaid Mr. *Enmity*. *He is a Rogue*, ſaid Mr. *Lyar*. *Hanging is too good for him*, ſaid Mr. *Cruelty*. *Lets diſpatch him out of the way*, ſaid Mr. *Hate-light*. Then ſaid Mr. *Implacable*, *Might I have all the World given me, I could not be reconciled to him*, therefore let us forthwith bring him in

K 2   *guilty*

guilty of death: And so they did, therefore he was presently Condemned, To be had from the place where he was, to the place from whence he came, and there to be put to the most cruel death that could be invented.

The cruel death of Faithful.

They therefore brought him out, to do with him according to their Law; and first they Scourged him, then they Buffetted him, then they Lanced his flesh with Knives; after that, they Stoned him with Stones, then prickt him with their Swords, and last of all they burned him to Ashes at the Stake. Thus came *Faithful* to his end. Now, I saw that there stood behind the multitude, a Chariot and a couple of Horses, waiting for *Faithful*, who (so soon as his adversaries had dispatched him) was taken up into it, and straightway was carried up through the Clouds, with sound of Trumpet, the nearest way to the Cœlestial Gate.

Christian is still alive.

But as for *Christian*, he had some respit, and was remanded back to prison, so he there remained for a space: But he that over-rules all things, having the power of their rage in his own hand, so wrought it about, that *Christian* for that time escaped them, and went his way.   *Well*

Well, Faithful, thou hast faithfully profest
Unto thy Lord: with him thou shalt be
bless;
When Faithless ones, with all their
vain delights,
Are crying out under their hellish plights
Sing, Faithful, sing; and let thy name
survive,
For though they kill'd thee, thou art yet
alive.

Now I saw in my Dream, that *Christian* went not forth alone, for there was one whose name was *Hope-ful*, (being made so by the beholding of *Christian* and *Faithful* in their words and behaviour, in their suffer-ings at the *fair*) who joyned himself unto him, and entering into a bro-therly covenant, told him that he would be his Companion. Thus one died to make Testimony to the Truth, and another rises out of his Ashes to be a Companion with *Christian*. This *Hopeful* also told *Christian*, that there were many more of the men in the *fair* that would take their time and follow after. *Christian has another Companion.*

There is more of the men of the fair will follow

So I saw that quickly after they were got out of the *fair*, they over-
took

took one that was going before them,
whose name was *By-ends*; so they said
to him, What Countrey-man, Sir?
and how far go you this way? He
told them, That he came from the
Town of *Fair-speech*, and he was going to the Cœlestial City, (but told
them not his name.)

From Fair-speech, *said* Christian; *is
there any that be good live there?*

By-ends. Yes, said *By-ends*, I hope.

Chr. *Pray Sir, what may I call you?*

By-ends. I am a Stranger to you,
and you to me; if you be going this
way, I shall be glad of your Company; if not, I must be content.

Chr. *This Town of* Fair-speech, *I
have heard of it, and, as I remember,
they say its a Wealthy place.*

Byends. Yes, I will assure you that
it is, and I have very many Rich
Kindred there.

Chr. *Pray who are your Kindred
there, if a man may be so bold?*

By-ends. To tell you Truth, I am a
Gentleman of good Quality; yet
my Great Grand-father was but a
Water-man, looking one way, and
Rowing another; and I got most of
my Estate by the same occupation.

Chr.

*They over-
take By-
ends.*

*By-ends
loth to tell
his name.*

Chr. Are you a Married man?

By-ends. Yes, and my Wife is a *The wife and Kindred of By-ends.* very Virtuous woman, the Daughter of a Virtuous woman: She was my Lady *Fainings* Daughter, therefore she came of a very Honourable Family, and is arrived to fuch a pitch of Breeding, that fhe knows how to carry it to all, even to Prince and Peafant. 'Tis true, we fomewhat differ *Where By-ends differs from others in Religion.* in Religion from thofe of the ftricter fort, yet but in two fmall points: Firft, we never ftrive againft Wind and Tide. Secondly, we are alwayes moft zealous when Religion goes in his Silver Slippers; we love much to walk with him in the Street, if the Sun fhines, and the people applaud it.

Then *Chriftian* ftept a little a to-fide to his Fellow *Hopeful*, faying, It runs in my mind that this is one *By-ends* of *Fair-fpeech*, and if it be he, we have as very a Knave in our Company, as dwelleth in all thefe parts. Then faid *Hopeful*, *Ask him, methinks he fhould not be afhamed of his name.* So *Chriftian* came up with him again, and faid, Sir, you talk as if you knew fomething more then all

K 4   the

the World doth, and if I take not
mark amifs, I deem I have half a gueff
of you: Is not your name Mr. *By-ends*
of *Fair-speech* ?

By-ends. That is not my name, but
indeed it is a Nick-name that is given
me by fome that cannot abide me, and
I muft be content to bear it as a reproach, as other good men have born
theirs before me.

Chr. *But did you never give an oc-
cafion to men to call you by this name?*

How By-ends got his name.

By-ends. Never, never! The worft
that ever I did to give them an oc-
cafion to give me this name, was,
That I had alwayes the luck to jump
in my Judgement with the prefent
way of the times, whatever it was,
and my chance was to get thereby ;
but if things are thus caft upon me,
let me count them a blefling, but let
not the malicious load me therefore
with reproach.

Chr. *I thought indeed that you was
the man that I had heard of, and to tell
you what I think, I fear this name belongs
to you more properly then you are willing we fhould think it doth.*

By-ends. Well, If you will thus imagine, I cannot help it. You fhall find
me

me a fair Company-keeper, if you *He defires to keep Company with Chriſtian.* will ſtill admit me your aſſociate.

Chr. If you will go with us, you muſt go againſt Wind and Tide, the which, I perceive, is againſt your opinion: You muſt alſo own Religion in his Rags, as well as when in his Silver Slippers, and ſtand by him too, when bound in Irons, as well as when he walketh the Streets with applauſe.

By-ends. You muſt not impoſe, nor Lord it over my Faith; leave me to my liberty, and let me go with you.

Chr. Not a ſtep further, unleſs you will do in what I propound, as we.

Then ſaid *By-ends*, I ſhall never deſert my old Principles, ſince they are harmleſs and profitable. If I may not go with you, I muſt do as I did before you overtook me, even go by my ſelf, untill ſome overtake me that will be glad of my Company.

Then *Chriſtian* and *Hopeful* outwent him, and went till they came *The eaſe that Pilgrims have is but little in this life.* at a delicate Plain, called *Eaſe*, where they went with much content; but that plain was but *narrow*, ſo they were quickly got over it. Now at the *Lucre Hill a dangerous Hill.* further ſide of that plain, was a little Hill called *Lucre*, and in that *Hill*

a

a *Silver-Mine*, which some of us that had formerly gone that way, becaufe of the rarity of it, had turned afide to fee, but going too near the brink of the pit, the ground being deceitful under them, broke, and they were flain; fome alfo had been maimed there, and could not to their dying day be their own men again.

Then I faw in my Dream, that a little off the road, over againft the *Silver-Mine*, ftood *Demas*, (Gentleman-like,) to call to Paffengers to come and fee: Who faid to *Chriftian* and his Fellow; Ho, turn afide hither, and I will fhew you a thing

Chr. *What thing fo deferving, as to turn us out of the way?*

De. Here is a Silver-*Mine*, and fome digging in it for Treafure; if you will come, with a little paines, you may richly provide for yourfelves.

Hopef. Then faid Hopeful, *Let us go fee.*

Chr. Not I, faid *Chriftian*; I have heard of this place before now, and how many have there been flain; and befides, that Treafure is a fnare to thofe that feek it, for it hindreth them in their Pilgrimage. Then *Chri-ftian*

Hopeful tempted to go, but Chriftian holds him back.

ſtian called to *Demas*, ſaying, *Is not the place dangerous? hath it not hin-* Hoſ. 4. 14 *dred many in their Pilgrimage?*

De. Not very dangerous, except to thoſe that are careleſs : but withal, he *bluſhed* as he ſpake.

Chr. Then ſaid *Chriſtian* to *Hopeful*, Let us not ſtir a ſtep, but ſtill keep on our way.

Hope. *I will warrant you, when* By-ends *comes up, if he hath the ſame invitation as we, he will turn in thither to ſee*.

Chr. No doubt, thereof, for his principles lead him that way, and a hundred to one but he dies there.

De. Then *Demas* called again, ſaying, But will you not come over and ſee?

Chr. Then *Chriſtian* roundly anſwered, ſaying, *Demas*, Thou art an Chriſtian roundeth up Demas 2 Tim. 4 10. Enemy to the right ways of the Lord of this way, and haſt been already condemned for thine own turning aſide, by one of his Majeſties Judges ; and why ſeekeſt thou to bring us into the like condemnation? Beſides, if we at all turn aſide, our Lord the King will certainly hear thereof; and will there put us to
ſhame,

shame, where we would stand with boldness before him.

Demas cried again, That he also was one of their fraternity; and that if they would tarry a little, he also himself would walk with them.

Chr. Then said *Christian*, What is thy name? is it not it by the which I have called thee?

Ce. Yes, my name is *Demas*, I am the son of *Abraham*.

Chr. I know you, *Gehazi* was your Great-Grandfather, and *Judas* your Father, and you have trod their steps. It is but a develish prank that thou usest: Thy Father was hanged for a Traitor, and thou deservest no better reward. Assure thy self, that when we come to the King, we will do him word of this thy behaviour. Thus they went their way.

2 Kings 5. 10. Mat. 26. 14, 15. chap. 27. 1, 2, 3. 4. 5.

By this time *By-ends* was come again within sight, and he at the first beck went over to *Demas*. Now whether he fell into the Pit, by looking over the brink thereof; or whether he went down to dig, or whether he was smothered in the bottom, by the damps that commonly arise, of these

By-ends goes over to Demas.

these things I am not certain: But
this I obferved, that he never was
feen again in the way.

By-ends *and Silver*-Demas *both agree*;
*One calls, the other runs, that he may
  be,*
*A fharer in his Lucre: fo thefe two
Take up in this world, and no fur-
  ther go.*

I faw then, that they went on *A River*
Pf. 65. 9.
Rev. 22.
Ezek. 47. their way to a pleafant River, which
David the King called the *River of
God*; but *John, The River of the water
of life:* Now their way lay juft upon
the bank of the River: here therefore *Chriftian* and his Companion
walked with great delight; They
drank alfo of the water of the River,
which was pleafant and enlivening to
their weary Spirits: befides, on the
banks of this River on either fide
were *green Trees*, that bore all manner
of Fruit; and the leaves of the Trees *Trees by
the River.
The Fruit
and leaves
of the Trees.* were good for Medicine; with the
Fruit of thefe Trees they were alfo
much delighted; and the leaves they
eat to prevent Surfeits, and other
Difeafes that are incident to thofe
                                  that

that heat their blood by Travel: On
either side of the River was also a
Meadow, curiously beautified with
Lilies; And it was green all the year
long. In this Meadow they lay down
and slept, for here they might *lie
down safely*. When they awoke, they
gathered again of the Fruit of the
Trees, and drank again of the Water
of the River: and then lay down
again to sleep. Thus they did several
days and nights.

*A Meadow
in which
they lie
down to
sleep.
Pf. 23.
Isa. 14. 30.*

> Behold ye how these Christal streams do
> glide
> (To comfort Pilgrims) by the High-
> way side;
> The Meadows green, besides their fra-
> grant smell,
> Yield dainties for them: And he that can
> tell
> What pleasant Fruit, yea Leaves, these
> Trees do yield,
> Will soon sell all, that he may buy this
> Field.

So when they were disposed to go
on (for they were not, as yet, at
their Journeys end) they eat and
drank, and departed.

Now I beheld in my Dream, that
they

they had not journied far, but the
River and the way, for a time parted. At which they were not a little
forry, yet they durſt not go out of
the way. Now the way from the
River was rough, and their feet tender by reaſon of their Travels; *So
the ſoul of the Pilgrims was much diſ-
couraged, becauſe of the way.* Where- *Numb.*
fore ſtill as they went on, they wiſhed *21. 4.*
for better way. Now a little before
them, there was on the left hand of
the Road, a *Meadow*, and a Stile to go
over into it, and that *Meadow* is called *By-Path-Meadow*. Then ſaid *Chri-*
ſtian to his fellow, If this Meadow li- *By-Path-*
eth along by our way ſide, lets go over *Meadow.*
into it. Then he went to the Stile to *One temp-*
tation does
ſee, and behold a Path lay along by *make way*
the way on the other ſide of the *for another*
fence. 'Tis according to my wiſh
ſaid *Chriſtian*, here is the eaſieſt going ; come good *Hopeful*, and lets us
go over.

Hop. *But how if this Path ſhould*
lead us out of the way? *Strong*
Chriſtians
Chr. That's not like, ſaid the o- *may lead*
ther ; look, doth it not go along by *weak ones*
the way ſide ? So *Hopeful*, being per- *out of the*
ſwaded by his fellow, went after him *way.*

over

over the Stile. When they were got over, and were got into the Path, they found it very easie for their feet; and withal, they looking before them, espied a Man walking as they did, (and his name was *Vain-confidence*) so they called after him, and asked him whither that way led? he said, To the Cœlestial Gate. Look, said *Christian*, did not I tell you so? by this you may see we are right: so they followed, and he went before them. But behold the night came on, and it grew very dark, so that they that were behind, lost the sight of him that went before.

He therefore that went before (*Vain-confidence* by name) not seeing the way before him, fell into a deep Pit, which was on purpose there made by the Prince of those grounds, to catch *vain-glorious* fools withall; and was dashed in pieces with his fall.

Isa. 9. 16.
A Pit to
catch the
vain glo-
rious in.

Now *Christian* and his fellow heard him fall. So they called, to know the matter, but there was none to answer, only they heard a groaning. Then said *Hopeful*, Where are we now? Then was his fellow silent firmly in miftrufting that he had led him out of the way. And now it began to rain, and thunder, and lighten in a very dreadful manner, and the water rofe amain.

Reafoning between Chriftian and Hopeful

Then *Hopeful* groaned in himfelf, faying, *Oh that I had kept on my way!*

Chr. Who could have thought that this path fhould have led us out of the way ?

Hope. *I was afraid on't at very firft, and therefore gave you that gentle caution. I would have fpoke plainer, but that you are older then I.*

Chr. Good Brother be not offended, I am forry I have brought thee out of the way, and that I have put thee into fuch eminent danger ; pray my Brother forgive me, I did not do it of an evil intent.

Chriftians repentance for leading of his Brother out of the way.

Hope. *Be comforted my Brother for I forgive thee; and believe too, that this fhall be for our good.*

Chr. I am glad I have with me a merciful Brother : But we muft not ftand thus, let's try to go back again.

Hope. *But good Brother let me go before.*

Chr. No, if you pleafe, let me go firft ; that if there be any danger, I

may

may be firſt therein, becauſe by that means we are both gone out of the way.

Hope. *No, ſaid* Hopeful, *you ſhall not go firſt, for your mind being troubled, may lead you out of the way again.* Then for their encouragement, they heard the voice of one ſaying, *Let thine heart be towards the High-*

Jer. 31. 21. *way, even the way that thou wenteſt,*

They are in danger of drowning as they go back.

turn again: But by this time the Waters were greatly riſen, by reaſon of which, the way of going back was very dangerous. (Then I thought that it is eaſier going out of the way when we are in, then going in when we are out.) Yet they adventured to go back; but it was ſo dark, and the flood was ſo high, that in their going back, they had like to have been drowned nine or ten times.

Neither could they, with all the skill they had, get again to the Stile that night. Wherefore, at laſt, lighting under a little ſhelter, they ſat down there till the day brake; but

They ſleep in the grounds of Giant Deſpair.

being weary, they fell aſleep. Now there was not far from the place where they lay, a *Caſtle*, called *Doubting Caſtle*, the owner whereof was

Giant

Giant *Despair*, and it was in his grounds they now were sleeping; wherefore he getting up in the morning early, and walking up and down in his Fields, caught *Christian* and *Hopeful* asleep in his grounds. Then with a *grim* and *surly* voice he bid them awake, and asked them whence they were? and what they did in his grounds? They told him, they were Pilgrims, and that they had loſt their way. Then ſaid the *Giant*, You have this night treſpaſſed on me, by trampling in, and lying on my grounds, and therefore you muſt go along with me. So they were forced to go, becauſe he was ſtronger then they. They alſo had but little to ſay, for they knew themſelves in a fault. The *Giant* therefore drove them before him, and put them into his Caſtle, into a very dark Dungeon, naſty and ſtinking to the ſpirit of theſe two men: Here then they lay, from *Wedneſday* morning till *Saturday* night, without one bit of bread, or drop of drink, or any light, or any to ask how they did. They were therefore here in evil caſe, and were far from friends and acquaintance. Now in this place,

He finds them in his ground, and carries them to Doubting Caſtle.

The Grievouſneſs of their Impriſonment

Pſ. 88. 18.

Christian had double sorrow, because 'twas through his unadvised haste that they were brought into this distress.

Well, on *Saturday* about midnight they began to *pray*, and continued in Prayer till almost break of day.

Now a little before it was day, good *Christian*, as one half amazed, brake out in this passionate Speech, *What a fool*, quoth he, *am I thus to lie in a stinking Dungeon, when I may as well walk at liberty?* I have a Key in my bosom, called *Promise*, that will, I am persuaded, open any Lock in *Doubting Castle*. Then said *Hopeful*, That's good News; good Brother pluck it out of thy bosom and try: Then *Christian* pulled it out of his bosom, and began to try at the Dungion door, whose bolt (as he turned the Key) gave back, and the door flew open with ease, and *Christian* and *Hopeful* both came out. Then he went to the outward door that leads into the *Castle yard*, and with his *Key* opened the door also. After he went to the *Iron* Gate, for that must be opened too, but that Lock went *damnable* hard, yet the Key did open it; then they thrust open the Gate

A Key in Christians, bosom called Promise, opens any Lock in Doubting Castle.

to

to make their escape with speed, but
that Gate, as it opened, made such
a creaking, that it waked *Giant Despair*, who hastily rising to pursue his
Prisoners, felt his Limbs to fail, so that
he could by no means go after them.
Then they went on, and came to the
Kings high way again, and so were
safe, because they were out of his
Jurisdiction.

Now when they were gone over
the Stile, they began to contrive with
themselves what they should do at
that Stile, to prevent those that should
come after, from falling into the
hands of *Giant Despair*. So they consented to erect there a Pillar, and to
engrave upon the side thereof, *Over
this Stile is the Way to* Doubting-*Castle,
which is kept by* Giant Despair *who,
despiseth the King of the Cælestial Countrey, and seeks to destroy his holy Pilgrims.*
Many therefore that followed after,
read what was written, and escaped
the danger. This done, they sang as
follows.

*Out of the way we went, and then we
    found
What 'twas to tread upon forbidden
    ground:*

And

And let them that come after them,
  care,
Left heedlesness makes them, as we,
  fare:
Left they, for trespassing, his prisoners
  are,
Whose Castle's Doubting, and whose
  name's Despair.

The de-
lectable
mountains.

They went then, till they came to the delectable Mountains, which Mountains belong to the Lord of that Hill, of which we have spoken before; so they went up to the Mountains, to behold the Gardens, and Orchards, the Vineyards, and Fountains of water, where also they drank, and washed themselves, and did freely eat of the Vineyards. Now there was on the tops of these Mountains, Shepherds feeding their flocks, and they stood by the high-way side. The Pilgrims therefore went to them, and leaning upon their staves, (as is common with weary Pilgrims, when they stand to talk with any by the way,) they asked, *Whose delectable Mountains are these? and whose be the sheep that feed upon them?*

They are refreshed in the mountains.

Shep.

Shep. These Mountains are *Immanuels Land,* and they are within sight of his City, and the sheep also are his, and he laid down his life for them.   John 10. 11

Chr. *Is this the way to the Cælestial City ?*

Shep. You are just in your way.

Chr. *How far is it thither ?*

Shep. Too far for any, but those that *shall* get thither indeed.

Chr. *Is the way safe, or dangerous ?*

Shep. Safe for those for whom it is to be safe, *but transgressors shall fall therein.*   Hof. 14. 9.

Chr. *Is there in this place any relief for Pilgrims that are weary and faint in the way ?*

Shep. The Lord of these Mountains hath given us a charge, *Not to be forgetful to entertain strangers:* There-   Heb. 13.
fore the good of the place is even   1, 2.
before you.

I saw also in my Dream, that when the Shepherds perceived that they were way-fairing men, they also put questions to them, (to which they made answer as in other places,) as, Whence came you? and, How got you into the way? and, By what means

L 4   have

have you so persevered them; but few of them that begin to come hither, do shew their face on the Mountains. But when the Shepherds heard their answers, being pleased therewith, they looked very lovingly upon them; and said, *Welcome to the delectable Mountains.*

The Shepherds, I say, whose names were, *Knowledge*, *Experience*, *Watchful*, and *Sincere*, took them by the hand, and had them to their Tents, and made them partake of that which was ready at present. They said moreover, We would that you should stay here a while, to acquaint with us, and yet more to solace yourselves with the good of these delectable Mountains. They told them, That they were content to stay; and so they went to their rest that night, because it was very late.

Then I saw in my Dream, that in the morning, the Shepherds called up *Christian* and *Hopeful* to walk with them upon the Mountains: So they went forth with them, and walked a while, having a pleasant prospect on every side. Then said the Shepherds one to another, Shall we shew these
Pilgrims

Pilgrims fome wonders? So when they had concluded to do it, they had them firft to the top of an Hill called *Errour*, which was very fteep on the furtheft fide, and bid them look down to the bottom. So *Chri-ftian* and *Hopeful* lookt down, and faw at the bottom feveral men dafhed all to pieces by a fall that they had from the top. Then faid *Chri-ftian*, What meaneth this? The Shepherds anfwered; Have you not heard of them that were made to err, by harkening to *Hymeneus*, and *Philetus*, as concerning the Faith of the Refurrection of the Body? They anfwered, Yes. Then faid the Shepherds, Thofe that you fee lie dafhed in pieces at the bottom of this Mountain, *are they*: and they have continued to this day unburied (as you fee) for an example to others to take heed how they clamber too high, or how they come too near the brink of this Mountain.

The Mountain of Errour.

Then I faw that they had them to the top of another Mountain, and the name of that is *Caution*; and bid them look a far off. Which when they did, they perceived as they thought,

Mount Caution.

thought, several men walking
down among the Tombs that
there. And they perceived that
men were blind, becaufe they ftumbled fometimes upon the Tombs, and
becaufe they could not get out from
among them. Then faid *Chriftian*,
What means this?

The Shepherds then anfwered,
Did you not fee a little below thefe
Mountains a *Stile* that led into a
Meadow on the left hand of this
way? They anfwered, Yes. Then faid
the Shepherds, From that Stile there
goes a Path that leads directly to
Doubting-Caftle, which is kept by
Giant Defpair; and thefe men (pointing to them among the Tombs)
came once on Pilgrimage, as you do
now, even till they came to that
fame *Stile*. And becaufe the right way
was rough in that place, they chofe
to go out of it into that Meadow,
and there were taken by Giant *Defpair*, and caft into *DoubtingCaftle*:
where, after they had a while been
kept in the Dungeon, he at laft did
put out their eyes, and led them a-
mong thofe Tombs, where he has
left them to wander to this very day;
that

that the saying of the wise Man might be fulfilled, *He that wandereth* Prov.21.16 *out of the way of understanding, shall remain in the Congregation of the dead.* Then *Christian* and *Hopeful* looked one upon another, with tears gushing out ; but yet said nothing to the Shepherds.

Then I saw in my Dream, that the Shepherds had them to another place, in a bottom, where was a door in the side of an Hill ; and they opened the door, and bid them look in. They looked in therefore, and saw that within it was very dark, and smoaky ; they also thought that they heard there a lumbring noise as of fire, and a cry of some tormented, and that they smelt the scent of Brimstone. Then said *Christian, What means this?* The Shepherds told them, saying, this is a By-way to Hell, a way that *A by-way* Hypocrites go in at ; namely, such as *to Hell.* sell their Birthright, with *Esau*: such as sell their Master, with *Judas*: such as blaspheme the Gospel with *Alexander*: and that lie and dissemble, with *Ananias* and *Saphira* his wife.

Hopef. Then said *Hopeful* to the Shepherds, *I perceive that these bad*

on

*on them, even every one, a shew of Pil-
grimage as we have now; had they
not?*

Shep. Yes, and held it a long time,
too.

Hopef. *How far might they go on
Pilgrimage in their day, since they notwithstanding were thus miserably cast
away?*

Shep. Some further, and some not
so far as these Mountains.

Then said the Pilgrims one to another, *We had need cry to the Strong for
strength.*

Shep. Ay, and you will have need
to use it when you have it, too.

By this time the Pilgrims had a
desire to go forwards, and the Shepherds a desire they should; so they
walked together towards the end of
the Mountains. Then said the Shepherds one to another, Let us here
shew to the Pilgrims the Gates of the
Cœlestial City, if they have skill
to look through our Perspective
Glass. The Pilgrims then lovingly
accepted the motion: So they had
them to the top of an high Hill called *Clear*, and gave them their Glass
to look. Then they essayed to look,

but

but the remembrance of that laſt
thing that the Shepheards had ſhewed them, made their hand ſhake,
by means of which impediment,
they could not look ſteddily through *The fruit*
the Glaſs; yet they thought they *of ſlaviſh*
ſaw ſomthing like the Gate, and alſo *fear.*
ſome of the Glory of the place,

> *Thus by the* Shepherds, *Secrets are*
>   *reveal'd,*
> *Which from all other men are kept con-*
>   *ceal'd:*
> *Come to the* Shepherds *then, if you*
>   *would ſee*
> *Things deep, things hid, and that my-*
>   *ſterious be.*

When they were about to depart,
one of the Shepherds gave them a
note of the way, Another of them,
bid them beware of the flatterer, The
third, *bid them take heed that they*
ſleep not upon the Inchanted Ground,
and the fourth, *bid them God ſpeed.*
So I awoke from my Dream.

And I ſlept, and Dreamed again,
and ſaw the ſame two Pilgrims going
down the Mountains along the High-
way towards the City. Now a little
below

below these Mountains, on the left hand, lieth the Countrey of Conceit, from which Countrey there comes into the way in which the Pilgrims walked, a little crooked Lane. Here therefore they met with a very brisk Lad, that came out of that Countrey; and his name was *Ignorance*. So *Chriſtian* asked him, *From what parts he came? and whither he was going?*

The Countrey of Conceit, out of which came Ignorance.

Ign. Sir, I was born in the Countrey that lieth off there, a little on the left hand; and I am going to the Cœleſtial City.

Chriſtian and Ignorance hath ſome talk.

Chr. *But how do you think to get in at the Gate, for you may find ſome difficulty there.*

Ign. As other good People do, ſaid he

Chr. *But what have you to ſhew at that Gate, that may cauſe that the Gate ſhould be opened unto you?*

Ign. I know my Lords will, and I have been a good Liver, I pay every man his own; I Pray, Faſt, pay Tithes, and give Alms, and have left my Countrey, for whither I am going.

Chr. *But thou cameſt not in at the Wicket-*

Wicket-gate, that is at the head of this way, thou camest in hither through that same crooked Lane, and therefore I fear, however thou mayeſt think of thy ſelf, when the reckoning day ſhall come, thou wilt have laid to thy charge, that thou art a Theif and a Robber, inſtead of admitance into the City.

Ignor. Gentlemen, ye be utter ſtrangers to me, I know you not, be content to follow the Religion of your Countrey, and I will follow the Religion of mine. I hope all will be well. And as for the Gate that you talk of, all the World knows that that is a great way off of our Countrey. I cannot think that any man in all our parts doth ſo much as know the way to it; nor need they matter whether they do or no, ſince we have, as you ſee, a fine pleaſant green Lane, that comes down from our Countrey the next way into it.

He ſaith to every one, that he is a fool.

When *Chriſtian* ſaw that the man was wiſe in his own conceit, he ſaid to *Hopeful*, whiſperingly, *There is more hopes of a fool then of him.* And ſaid moreover, *When he that is a fool walketh by the way, his wiſdom faileth him, and he ſaith to every one that*

Pr. 26. 12

Eccl. 10. 3.

How to carry it to a fool. that he is a fool. What, shall we further with him? or out-go him at present? and so leave him to think of what he hath heard already; and then stop again for him afterwards, and see if by degrees we can do any good of him?

Let Ignorance a little while now muse
On what is said, and let him not refuse
Good Counsel to imbrace, lest he remain
Still Ignorant of what's the chiefest gain.
God saith, Those that no understanding
    have,
(Although he made them) them he will
    not save.

Hop. It is not good, I think, to say all to him at once, let us pass him by, if you will, and talk to him anon, *even as he is able to bear it.*

So they both went on, and Igno-rance he came after. Now when they had passed him a little way, they entered into a very dark Lane, where they met a man whom seven Matt. 12. Devils had bound with seven strong 45. Prov. Cords, and were carrying of him 5. 22. back *to the door* that they saw in the side of the Hill. Now good *Christian*
    began

began to tremble, and so did *Hopeful* his Companion: Yet as the Devils led away the man, *Christian* looked to see if he knew him, and he thought it might be one *Turn-away* that dwelt in the *Town* of *Apostacy*. But he did not perfectly see his face, for he did hang his head like a Thief that is found: But being gone past, *Hopeful* looked after him, and espied on his back a Paper with this Inscription, *Wanton Professor, and damnable Apostate*. Then said *Christian* to his Fellow, Now I call to remembrance that which was told me of a thing that happened to a good man hereabout. The name of the man was *Little-Faith*, but a good man, and he dwelt in the Town of *Sincere*. The thing was this; at the entering in of this passage there comes down from *Broad-way-gate* a Lane called *Dead-mans-lane*; so called, because of the Murders that are commonly done there. And this *Little-Faith* going on Pilgrimage, as we do now, chanced to sit down there and slept. Now there happened, at that time, to come down that *Lane* from *Broad-way-gate* three Sturdy Rogues, and

The destruction of one Turn-away.

Christian telleth his Companion a story of Little-Faith.

Broadway-gate.
Deadmans Lane.

M   their

their names were Faint-heart, Mistrust, and Guilt, (three brothers) and they espying Little-faith where he was, came galloping up with speed: Now the good man was just awaked from his sleep, and was getting up to go on his Journey. So they came all up to him, and with threatning Language bid him stand. At this, Little faith lookt as white as a Clout, and had neither power to fight nor flie. Then said Faint-heart, Deliver thy Purse; but he making no haste to do it, (for he was loth to lose his Money,) Mistrust ran up to him, and thrusting his hand into his Pocket, pull'd out thence a bag of Silver. Then he cried out, Thieves, thieves. With that, Guilt with a great Club that was in his hand, strook Little-Faith on the head, and with that blow fell'd him flat to the ground, were he lay bleeding as one that would bleed to death. All this while the Thieves stood by: But at last, they hearing that some were upon the Road, and fearing lest it should be one Great-grace that dwells in the City of Good-confidence, they betook themselves to their heels, and left this good man to shift for him-

Little-faith robbed by Faint-heart, Mistrust and Guilt.

They get away his Silver, and knocks him down.

himſelf. Now after a while, *Little-
faith* came to himſelf, and getting
up, made ſhift to ſcrabble on his way.
This was the ſtory.

Hopef. *But did they take from him
all that ever he had?*

Chriſt. No: The place where his
Jewels were, they never ranſak't, ſo
thoſe he kept ſtill; but as, I was told,
the good man was much afflicted for
his loſs. For the Thieves got moſt of
his ſpending Money. That which
they got not (as I ſaid) were Jewels,
alſo he had a little odd Money left,
but *ſcarce* enough to bring him to
his Journeys end; nay, (if I was not
mis-informed) he was forced to beg
as he went, to keep himſelf alive,
(for his Jewels he might not ſell.)But
beg, and do what he could, *be went*
(as we ſay) *with many a hungry belly,*
the moſt part of the reſt of the
way.

Hopef. *But is it not a wonder they got
not from him his Certificate, by which he
was to receive his admittance at the
Cœleſtial gate?*

Chr. No, they got not that:
though thy miſt it not through any
good cunning of his, for he being

*Little-
faith loſt
not his beſt
things.*

1 Pet. 4.
18.

*Little-
faith forced
to beg to
his Jour-
neys end.*

M 2　　　　diſ-

He kept not his best things by his own cunning.
2 Tim. 1. 14.
dismayed with their coming upon him, had neither power nor skill to hide any thing; so 'twas more by good Providence then by his Indeavour, that they mist of that good thing.

Hopef. *But it must needs be a comfort to him, that they got not this Jewel from him.*

2 Pet. 1. 9.
Chr. It might have been great comfort to him, had he used it as he should; but they that told me the story, said, That he made but little use of it all the rest of the way; and that because of the dismay that he had in their taking away of his Money: indeed he forgot it a great part of the rest of the Journey; and besides, when at any time, it came into his mind, and he began to be comforted therewith, then would fresh thoughts of his loss come again upon him, and those thoughts would swallow up all.

Hope. *Alas poor Man! this could not but be a great grief unto him.*

He is pittied by both.
Chr. Grief! Ay, a grief indeed! would it not a been so to any of us, had we been used as he, to be Robbed and wounded too, and that in a strange

strange place, as he was? 'Tis a
wonder he did not die with grief,
poor heart! I was told, that he scat-
tered almost all the rest of the way
with nothing but doleful and bitter
complaints.   Telling also to all that
over-took him, or that he over-took
in the way as he went, where he was
Robbed, and how; who they were
that did it, and what he lost; how
he was wounded, and that he hardly
escaped with life.

*Hope. But 'tis a wonder that his
necessities did not put him upon* selling,
*or pawning some of his Jewels, that he
might have wherewith to relieve himself in his Journey.*

Chr. Thou talkest like one upon
whose head is the Shell to this very Christian
day: For what should he *pawn* them? *chibbeth*
or to whom should he sell them? In *his fellow
for unadver-*
all that Countrey where he was *sed speak-*
Robbed, his Jewels were not accoun-*ing.*
ted of, nor did he want that relief
which could from thence be administred to him; besides, had his Jewels
been missing at the Gate of the Coelestial City, he had (and that he
knew well enough) been excluded
from an Inheritance there; and that

M 3   would

would have been worfe to him, the appearance and villany of a thoufand Thieves.

Hope. *Why art thou fo tart my Brother?* *Efau* fold his Birth-right, and that for a mefs of Pottage; and that Birth-right was his greateft Jewel: and if he, why might not Little-Faith do fo too?

Chr. *Efau* did fell his Birth-right indeed, and fo do many befides; and by fo doing, exclude themfelves from the chief bleffing, as alfo that *Caytiff* did. But you muft put a difference betwixt *Efau* and *Little-Faith,* and alfo betwixt their Eftates. *Efau's* Birth-right was Typical, but *Little-faith's* Jewels were not fo. *Efau's* belly was his God, but *Little-faith's* belly was not fo. *Efau's* want lay in his flefhly appetite, *Little-faith's* did not fo. Befides, *Efau* could fee no further then to the fulfilling of his Lufts, *For I am at the point to dye,* faid he, *and what good will this Birth-right do me?* But *Little-faith,* though it was his lot to have but a *littlefaith,* was by his *little faith* kept from fuch extravagancies; and made to *fee* and *prize* his Jewels more, then to fell them,

Heb. 12. 16.

A difcourfe about Efau and Little-Faith.

Efau was ruled by his lufts.

Gen. 25: 32.

them, as *Esau* did his Birth-right. *Esau never had faith*

You read not any where that *Esau*
had *faith*, no not so much as a *little*:
Therefore no marvel, if where the
flesh only bears sway (as it will in
that Man where *no* faith is to resist)
if he sells his *Birth-right* , and his
Soul and all, and that to the Devil of
Hell ; for it is with such, as it is with
the Ass, *Who in her occasions cannot be* Jer. 2. 24.
turned away. When their minds are
set upon their Lusts, they will have
them what ever they cost. But *Little-* *Little-*
faith was of another temper , his *faith could not live*
mind was on things Divine ; his *upon Esaus*
livelyhood was upon things that *Pottage.*
were Spiritual , and from above ;
Therefore to what end should he that
is of such a temper sell his Jewels,
(had there been any that would have
bought them) to fill his mind with
empty things ? Will a man give a
penny to fill his belly with Hay ? or *A compa-*
can you persuade the *Turtle-dove* to *rison be-* *tween the*
live upon Carrion, like the *Crow* ? *Turtle-*
Though *faithless* ones, can for carnal *dove and*
Lusts, pawn, or morgage, or sell what *the Crow.*
they have, and themselves out right
to boot ; yet they that have *faith*,
saving faith, though but a *little* of it,
M 4 cannot

cannot do fo. Here therefore,
Brother, is thy miſtake.

Hopef. *I acknowledge it; but
your ſevere reflection had almoſt made
me angry*

Chr. Why, I did but compare thee
to ſome of the Birds that are of the
briſker ſort, who will run to and
fro in troden paths with the ſhell upon their heads: but paſs by that, and
conſider the matter under debate,
and all ſhall be well betwixt thee and
me.

Hopef. *But* Chriſtian, *Theſe three
fellows, I am perſwaded in my heart, are
but a company of Cowards: would they
have run elſe, think you, as they did,
at the noiſe of one that was coming on*

the road? Why did not Little-faith

*pluck up a great heart? He might, me-
thinks, have ſtood one bruſh with them,
and have yielded when there had been
no remedy.*

Chr. That they are Cowards, many
have ſaid, but few have found it ſo

in the time of Trial. As for *a great*

heart, Little-faith had none; and I
perceive by thee, my Brother, hadſt

thou been the Man concerned, thou

art but for a bruſh, and then to yield.

And

Hopeful
ſwaggers.

No great
heart for
God where
there is but
little faith

And verily, fince this is the height of
thy Stomach now they are at a
diftance from us, fhould they appear
to thee, as they did to him, they
might put thee to fecond thoughts.

We know more courage when out, then when we are in.

But confider again, they are but
Journey-men Thieves, they ferve under the King of the Bottomlefs pit;
who, if need be, will come to their
aid himfelf, and his voice is *as the*
roaring of a Lion. I my felf have
been Ingaged as this *Little-faith* was,
and I found it a terrible thing. Thefe
three Villains fet upon me, and I beginning like a *Chriftian* to refift,
they gave but a call, and in came
their Mafter: I would as the faying is, have given my life for a penny; but that, as God would have it,
I was cloathed with Armour of proof.
Ay, and yet though I was fo harnef-
fed, I found it hard work to quit my
felf like a man; no man can tell what
in that Combat attends us, but he
that hath been in the Battle himfelf.

Pfal. 5. 8. Chriftian tells his own expe- rience in this cafe.

Hopef. *Well, but they ran you fee,*
when they did but fuppofe that one
Great-Grace *was in the way.*

Chr. True, they often fled, both
they and their Mafter, when *Great-*
grace

grace hath but appeared, and no marvel, for he is *the Kings Champion*. But I tro, you will put some difference between *Little-faith* and the *Kings Champion*; all the Kings Subjects are not his Champions: nor can they, when tried, do such feats of War as he. Is it meet to think that a little child fhould handle *Goliah* as *David* did? or that there fhould be the ftrength of an *Ox* in a *Wren*? Some are ftrong, fome are weak, fome have *great* faith, fome have *little*: this man was one of the weak, and therefore he went to the walls.

Hopef. *I would it had been* Great-grace, *for their fakes.*

Chr. If it had been he, he might have had his hands full: For I muft tell you, That though *Great-grace* is excellent good at his Weapons, and has and can, fo long as he keeps them at Swords point, do well enough with them: yet if they get within him, even *Faint-heart*, *Miftruft*, or the other, it fhall go hard but they will throw up his heels. And when a man is down, you know what can he do.

Who fo looks well upon *Great-graces*

grace's face, shall see those Scars and
Cuts there, that shall easily give de-
monstration of what I say.   Yea once
I heard he should say, (and that when
he was in the Combat) *We despaired
even of life* : How did these sturdy
Rogues and their Fellows make *David* groan, mourn, and roar? Yea
Heman, and *Hezekiah* too, though
Champions in their day, were forced
to bestir them, when by these af-
saulted; and yet, that notwithstanding, they had their Coats soundly
brushed by them. *Peter* upon a time
would go try what he could do; but,
though some do say of him that he
is the Prince of the Apostles, they
handled him so, that they made him
at last afraid of a sorry Girle.

Besides, their King is at their
Whistle, he is never out of hearing;
and if at any time they be put to
the worst, he, if possible, comes in to
help them: And, of him it is said, Job. 41. 26
*The Sword of him that layeth at him
cannot hold the Spear, the Dart, nor the
Habergeon*; *he esteemeth Iron as Straw*, Levia-
and Brass as rotten Wood. The Arrow thans stur-
cannot make him flie, Slingstones are diness.
turned with him into stubble, Darts are
counted

counted as *stubble*, *be laugheth at the shaking of a Spear*. What can a man do in this case? 'Tis true, if a man could at every turn have *Jobs* Horse, and had skill and courage to ride him, he might do notable things. *For* **his neck is clothed with Thunder, he will not be afraid as the Grashoper, the glory of his Nostrils is terrible, he paweth in the Valley, rejoyceth in his strength, and goeth out to meet the armed men. He mocketh at fear, and is not affrighted, neither turneth back from the Sword. The quiver rattleth against him, the glittering Spear, and the shield. He swalloweth the ground with fiercenefs and rage, neither believeth he that it is the found of the Trumpet. He faith among the Trumpets, Ha, ha; and he smelleth the Battel a far off, the thundring of the Captains, and the shoutings.**

The excellent mettle that is in Jobs Horse

Iob 39. 19

But for such footmen as thee and I are, let us never defire to meet with an enemy, nor vaunt as if we could do better, when we hear of others that they have been foiled, nor be tickled at the thoughts of our own manhood, for such commonly come by the worft when tried. Witnefs *Peter*, of whom I made

made mention before. He would
swagger, Ay he would: He would, as
his vain mind prompted him to say,
do better, and stand more for his
Master, then all men: But who so
foiled, and run down by these *Vil-*
lains, as he?

When therefore we hear that such
Robberies are done on the Kings
High-way, two things become us
to do; first to go out Harnessed, and
to be sure *to take a Shield with us*: For
it was for want of that, that he that
laid so lustily at *Leviathan* could not
make him yield. For indeed, if that
be wanting, he fears us not at all.
Therefore he that had skill, hath said,
Above all take the Shield of Faith, Eph. 6. 16.
wherewith ye shall be able to quench all
the fiery darts of the wicked.

'Tis good also that we desire of the *Tis gratis*
King a Convoy, yea that he will go *have a*
with us himself. This made *David* Convoy.
rejoyce when in the Valley of the
shaddows of death; and *Moses* was Ex. 33. 15.
rather for dying where he stood, then
to go one step without his God. O
my Brother, if he will but go along Psal. 3. 6,
with us, what need we be afraid of 6, 7, 8.
ten thousands that shall set them- Psal. 27.1,
selves 2, 3

selves against us, but without...

the proud *helpers fall under the...*

I for my part have been in the ...
before now, and though (through ...
goodnefs of him that is beft) I am
as you fee alive: yet I cannot boaft
of my manhood. Glad fhall I be, if I
meet with no more fuch brunts,
though I fear we are not got beyond
all danger. However, fince the Lion
and the Bear hath not as yet devou-
red me, I hope God will alfo deliver us from the next uncircumcifed
Philiftine.

Poor Little-faith ! *Haft been among the*
    Thieves!
Waft robb'd! Remember this, Who fo
    believes
And gets more faith, fhall then a Vi-
    ctor be
Over ten thoufand, elfe fcarce over
    three.

So they went on, and *Ignorance* followed. They went then till they
came at a place where they faw a
way put it felf into their *way*, and
seemed withal, to lie as ftraight as
the way which they fhould go; and
         here

here they knew not which of the two
to take, for both feemed ftraight before them ; therefore here they ftood
ftill to confider.   And as they were
thinking about the way, behold a
man black of flefh, but covered with
a very light Robe, came to them and
asked them, Why they ftood there ?
They anfwered, They were going to
the Cœleftial City, but knew not
which of thefe ways to take.   Follow me, faid the man, it is thither
that I am going . So they followed
him in the way that but now came *Chriftian*
into the road, which by degrees turn- *and his*
ed, and turned them fo from the *fellow de-*
City that they defired to go to, *luded.*
that in little time their faces were
turned away from it ; yet they followed him.   But by and by, before
they were aware, he led them both
within the compafs of a Net, in
which they were both fo entangled *They are*
that they knew not what to do ; and *taken in a*
with that, the *white Robe fell off the* *Net.*
black mans back ; then they faw where
they were.   Wherefore there they
lay crying fometime, for they could
not get themfelves out.

    Chr. Then faid *Chriftian* to his fel-
low.

They be-
wail their
condition.

Pro. 29. 5. low, Now do I see my
errour. Did not the Shepherds bid
us beware of the flatterers?
the saying of the Wise man,
have found it this day: *A man
flattereth his Neighbour, spreadeth
a
Net for his feet.*

Hopef. They also gave us a note
of directions about the way, for our
more sure finding thereof: but therein we have also forgotten to read,
and have not kept our selves from
the Paths of the destroyer. Here
David was wiser than wee; for saith

Psal. 17. 4.

A shining
one comes
to them
with a
whip in
hand. he, *Concerning the works of men, by
the word of thy lips, I have kept me
from the Paths of the destroyer.* Thus
they lay bewailing themselves in the
Net. At last they espied a shining
One coming towards them, with a
whip of small cord in his hand. When
he was come to the place where they
were, He asked them whence they
came? and what they did there?
They told him, That they were poor
Pilgrims going to *Sion*, but were
led out of their way, by a black man,
cloathed in white, who bid us, said
they, follow him; for he was going thither too. Then said he with the
Whip

Whip; it is *Flatterer*, a false Apoſtle, that hath transformed himſelf into an Angel of light So he rent the Net and let the men out. Then ſaid he to them, Follow me, that I may ſet you in your way again ; ſo he led them back to the way, which they had left to follow the *Flatterer*. Then he asked them, ſaying, Where did you lie the laſt night ? They ſaid with the Shepherds upon the delectable Mountains. He asked them then, If they had not of them Shepherds *a note of direction for the way ?* They anſwered, Yes. But did you, ſaid he when you was at a ſtand, pluck out and read your note? They anſwered, No. He asked them why ? They ſaid they forgot He asked moreover, If the Shepherds did not bid them beware of the *Flatterer* ? They anſwered, Yes : But we did not imagine, ſaid they, that this fine-ſpoken man had been he.

Then I ſaw in my Dream, that he commanded them to *lie down* ; which when they did, he chaſtized them ſore, to teach them the good way wherein they ſhould walk ; and as he chaſtized them, heſaid, *As many*

Pro. 29. 5.
Da. 11. 32.
2 Cor. 11.
13, 14.

They are examined and convicted of forgetful nels.

Deceivers fine ſpoken.
Ro, 16. 18.

Deu. 25. 2.
2 Chron. 6.
26, 27.

Rev, 3. 19

N   as

They are, as I *know, I *ra...
*white, and zealous therefore, and *...
*sent on done, he bids them go on *...
*their way. and take good heed to the o*ther* directions of the Shepherds. So *they*
thanked him for all his kindness, *and*
went softly along the right way.

> Come hither, you that walk along *the*
>   way ;
> See how the Pilgrims fare, that go *a-*
>   stray !
> They catched are in an intangling Net,
> 'Cause they good Counsel lightly *did*
>   forget :
> 'Tis true, they rescu'd were, but *yet*
>   you see
> They're scourg'd to boot : Let this *your*
>   caution be.

Now after a while, they perceived
afar off, one coming softly and alone,
all along the High-way to meet
them. Then said *Christian* to his
fellow, Yonder is a man with his
back toward *Sion*, and he is coming
to meet us.

Hopef. I see him, let us take heed
to our selves now, lest he should
prove a *Flatterer* also. So he drew
nearer

nearer and nearer, and at laſt came
up unto them. His name was *Atheiſt*, *The Atheiſt*
and he asked them whether they *meets them,*
were going.

Chr. *We are going to the Mount*
Sion.

Then *Atheiſt* fell into a very great *He Laughs*
Laughter. *at them.*

Chr. *What is the meaning of your*
Laughter ?

Atheiſt. I laugh to ſee what ignorant perſons you are, to take upon
you ſo tedious a Journey ; and yet are
like to have nothing but your travel
for your paines.

Chr. *Why man ? Do you think we* *They rea-*
ſhall not be received ? *ſon toge-*
ther.

Atheiſt. Received! There is no ſuch
place as you Dream of, in all this
World.

Chr. *But there is in the World to*
come.

Atheiſt. When I was at home in
mine own Countrey, I heard as you
now affirm ; and from that hearing
went out to ſee, and have been ſeek-
ing this City this twenty years : But Jer. 2a. 15.
find no more of it, then I did the firſt Ec. 10, 15.
day I ſet out.

Chr. *We have both heard and be-*
N 2 *lieve*

Atheist. Had not I, when ...
believed, I had not come this ...
feek : But finding none, (and ...

The Athe-
iſt takes up
his content
in this
World.
ſhould, had there been ſuch a ...
to be found, for I have gone to ſeek
it further then you *)* I am going ...
again, and will ſeek to refreſh ...
ſelf with the things that I then ...
away, for hopes of that which I ...
ſee is not.

Chriſtian
proveth his
Brother.
Chr. Then ſaid *Chriſtian* to *Hope-*
ful his Fellow, *Is it true which this*
man hath ſaid ?

Hopefuls
gracious
anſwer
Hopef. Take heed, he is one of the
Flatterers ; remember what it hath
coſt us once already for our harkning
to ſuch kind of Fellows. What ! no
Mount *Sion !* Did we not ſee from

2.Cor.5.7.
the delectable Mountains the Gate
of the City ? Alſo, are we not now
to walk by Faith ? Let us go on, ſaid
Hopeful, leſt the man with the Whip
overtakes us again.

You ſhould have taught me that
Leſſon, which I will round you in the

Prov. 19.
27.
Heb. 10.
39.
ears withall ; *Ceaſe, my Son, to hear the*
Inſtruction that cauſeth to err from the
words of knowledge. I ſay my Brother,
ceaſe

ceafe to hear him, and let us believe
to the faving of the Soul.

Chr. *My Brother, I did not put the
queftion to thee, for that I doubted of the
Truth of our belief my felf: But to prove* *A fruit of*
thee, and to fetch from thee a fruit of *an honeft*
the honefty of thy heart. *As for this* *heart.*
man, I know that he is blinded by the god
of this World: Let thee and I go on,
knowing that we have belief of the
Truth, and no lie is of the Truth. 1 John 2. 11

Hopef. Now do I rejoyce in hope
of the Glory of God: So they turned
away from the man; and he, Laughing at them, went his way.

I faw then in my Dream, that they *They are*
went till they came into a certain *come to the*
Countrey, whofe Air naturally ten- *inchanted*
ded to make one drowfie, if he *ground*
came a ftranger into it. And here
Hopeful began to be very dull and
heavy of fleep, wherefore he faid unto *Chriftian*, I do now begin to grow
fo drowfie, that I can fcarcely hold *Hopeful*
up mine eyes; let us lie down here *begins to*
and take one Nap. *be drowfie*

Chr. *By no means*, faid the other, *Chriftian*
left fleeping, we never awake more. *keeps him*
Hopef. Why my Brother? fleep is *awake*
fweet to the Labouring man; we

may

... may be refreshed if we ...

Chr. Do you not remember ... of the *Shepherds* bid us beware ... Inchanted ground? He meant by that

1 Thes. 5. 6 that we should beware of sleeping, where-fore let us not sleep as do others, but let us watch and be sober.

He is   *Hopef.* I acknowledge my self in
thankful. fault, and had I been here alone, I had by sleeping run the danger of death. I see it is true that the wise

Eccl. 4. 9. man saith, *Two are better then one.* Hitherto hath thy Company been my mercy; *and thou shalt have a good reward for thy labour.*

To prevent   *Chr. Now then*, said *Christian,*
drowsiness *to prevent drowsiness in this place, let*
they fall to *let us fall into good discourse.*
good dis-
course.   *Hopef.* With all my heart, said the other.

Good dis-   *Chr. Where shall we begin?*
course pre-   *Hopef.* Where God began with us.
vents drow- But do you begin, if you please.
siness.

When Saints do sleepy grow, let them come hither,
And hear how these two Pilgrims talk together:
Yea, let them learn of them, in any wise,
Thus to keep ope their drowsie slumbring eyes.   *Saints*

Saints fellowship, if it be manag'd well,
Keeps them awake, and that in spite of
bell.

Chr. Then *Christian* began and said,
I will ask you a question. How came you
to think at first of doing as you do now?

Hopef. Do you mean, How came
I at first to look after the good of my
Soul *?*

Chr. Yes, that is my meaning.

Hopef. I continued a great while
in the delight of those things which
were seen and sold at our *fair*; things
which, as I believe now, would have
(had I continued in them still) drownded me in perdition and destruction.

Chr. What things were they ?

Hopef. All the Treasures and Riches
of the World. Also I delighted much in
Rioting, Revelling, Drinking, Swearing , Lying, Uncleannefs, Sabbath-
breaking, and what not , that tended to destroy the Soul.   But I found
at last, by hearing and considering of
things that are Divine, which indeed
I heard of you , as also of beloved
Faithful, that was put to death for Rom. 6. 21
his Faith and good-living in *Vanity-* 22, 23.
fair, That the end of these things is Eph. 5. 6.
    N 4   *death.*

death. And that for thes . . . the wrath of God cometh upon . . . children of difobedience.

Chr. _And did you prefently fall into the power of this conviction?_

Hopef. No, I was not willing pre-fently to know the evil of fin, nor the damnation that follows upon the commiffion of it, but endeavoured, when my mind at firft began to be fhaken with the word, to fhut mine eyes againft the light thereof.

Chr. _But what was the caufe of your carrying of it thus to the firft workings of Gods bleffed Spirit upon you?_

Hopef. The caufes were, 1. I was ignorant that this was the work of God upon me. I never thought that by awaknings for fin, God at firft be-gins the converfion of a finner. 2. Sin was yet very fweet to my flefh, and I was loth to leave it. 3. I could not tell how to part with mine old Com-panions, their prefence and actions were fo defirable unto me. 4. The hours in which convictions were up-on me, were fuch troublefome and fuch heart-affrighting hours, that I could not bear, no not fo much as the remembrance of them upon my heart.

Chr

Chr. *Then as it seems, sometimes you got rid of your trouble.*

Hopef. Yes verily, but it would come into my mind again, and then I should be as bad, nay worse, then I was before.

Chr. *Why, what was it that brought your sins to mind again?*

Hopef. Many things, As,

1. If I did but meet a good man in the Streets; or,

2. If I have heard any read in the Bible; or,

3. If mine Head did begin to Ake; or,

4. I were told that some of my Neighbours were sick; or,

5. If I heard the Bell Toull for some that were dead; or,

6. If I thought of dying my self; or,

7. If I heard that suddain death happened to others.

8. But especially, when I thought of my self, that I must quickly come to Judgement.

Chr. *And could you at any time with ease get off the guilt of sin when by any of these wayes it came upon you?*

Hopef. No, not latterly, for then they got faster hold of my Conscience

... And then, it ...
of going back to sin ...
mind was turned against it ...
be double torment to me. ...

Chr. *And how did you do then?*

Hopef. I thought I must endeavour to mend my life, for else
thought I, I am sure to be damned.

Chr. *And did you indeavour to
mend?*

Hopef. Yes, and fled from, not
only my sins, but sinful Company
too; and betook me to Religious
Duties, as Praying, Reading, weeping for Sin, speaking Truth to my
Neighbours, &c. These things I did
with many others, too much here to
relate.

Chr. *And did you think your self well
then?*

Hopef. Yes, for a while; but at the
last my trouble came tumbling upon
me again, and that over the neck of
all my Reformations.

Chr. *How came that about, since
you was now Reformed?*

Hopef. There were several things
brought it upon me, especially such
Iſa. 64. 6. sayings as these; *All our righteousneſſes*
Gala.2.16. *are as filthy rags. By the works of the*
Law

Law no man shall be justified. When you have done all things say, We are un- Luk.17.10 *profitable :* with many more the like. From whence I began to reason with my self thus: If *all* my righteousnesses are filthy rags, if by the deeds of the Law, *no* man can be justified; And if, when we have done *all*, we are yet unprofitable : Then tis but a folly to think of Heaven by the Law. I further thought thus: If a Man runs an 100*l.* into the Shop-keepers debt, and after that shall pay for all that he shall fetch, yet his old debt stands still in the Book uncrossed; for the which the Shop-keeper may sue him, and cast him into Prison till he shall pay the debt.

Chr. *Well, and how did you apply this to your self?*

Hopef. Why, I thought thus with my self; I have by my sins run a great way into Gods Book, and that my now reforming will not pay off that score ; therefore I should think still under all my present amendments, But how shall I be freed from that damnation that I have brought my self in danger of by my former transgressions?

Chr.

Chr. A very good... pray go on.

Hope. Another thing that ...bled me, even since my late a...ments, is, that if I look narrow... the beſt of what I do now, I ſtill ...new ſin, mixing it ſelf with the ... of that I do. So that now I am forc...to conclude, that notwithſtanding my former fond conceits of my ſe... and duties, I have committed ſin ... nough in one duty to ſend me to Hell, though my former life had been faultleſs.

Chr. And what did you do then?

Hopef. Do! I could not tell what to do, till I brake my mind to *Faith*-*ful*; for he and I were well acquain-ted: And he told me, That unleſs I could obtain the righteouſneſs of a man that never had ſinned, neither mine own, nor all the righteouſneſs of the World could ſave me.

Chr. And did you think he ſpake true?

Hopef. Had he told me ſo when I was pleaſed and ſatisfied with mine own amendments, I had cal-led him Fool for his pains: but now, ſince I ſee my own infirmity, and the

the fin that cleaves to my beft performance, I have been forced to be of his opinion.

Chr. *But did you think, when at firft be fuggefted it to you, that there was fuch a man to be found, of whom it might juftly be faid, That be never committed fin?*

Hopef. I muft confefs the words at firft founded ftrangely, but after a little more talk and company with him, I had full conviction about it.

Chr. *And did you ask him what man this was, and how you muft be juftified by him?*

Hope. Yes, and he told me it was the Lord Jefus, that dwelleth on the right hand of the moft High: And thus, faid he, you muft be juftified by him, even by trufting to what he hath done by himfelf in the days of his flefh, and fuffered when he did hang on the Tree. I asked him further, How that mans righteoufnefs could be of that efficacy, to juftifie another before God? And he told me, He was the mighty God, and did what he did, and died the death alfo, not for himfelf, but for us; to whom his doings, and the worthinefs of them

Heb. 10,
Rom. 4.
Col. 1.
1 Pet.

them fhould be imputed, ...
on him.

Chr. *And what did you* ...

Hope. I made my objections ...
my believing, for that I thought ...
was not willing to fave me.

Chr. *And what faid* Faithful *to you*
then?

Hopef. He bid me go to him and
fee: Then I faid, It was prefumption:
Mat.11.28 but he faid, No: for I was invited to
come. Then he gave me a book of Je-
fus his inditing, to incourage me the
more freely to come: And he faid
concerning that Book, That every
jot and tittle there of ftood firmer
Matt.24.35 then Heaven and earth. Then I asked
him, What I muft do when I came?
Pf. 95. 6. and he told me, I muft intreat upon
Dan. 6. 10. my knees with all my heart and foul,
Jer. 29. 12, the Father to reveal him to me. Then
13. I asked him further, How I muft
make my fupplication to him? And
he faid, Go, and thou fhalt find him
Ex.at 22. upon a mercy-feat, where he fits all
Lev. 16. 2. the year long, to give pardon and
Nu. 7. 89. forgivenefs to them that come. I
Heb. 4. 6. told him that I knew not what to
fay when I came: and he bid me fay
to this effect, *God be merciful to me a*
finner.

sinner, and make me to know and believe
in *Jesus Christ*; for I see that if his
righteousness had not been, or I have not
*faith in that righteousness, I am utterly
cast away: Lord, I have heard that thou
art a merciful God, and hast ordained
that thy Son Jesus Christ should be the
Saviour of the World; and moreover,
that thou art willing to bestow him upon
such a poor sinner as I am, (and I am
a sinner indeed) Lord take therefore
this opportunity, and magnifie thy grace
in the Salvation of my soul, through
thy Son Jesus Christ*, Amen.

Chr. *And did you do as you were
bidden ?*

Hopef. Yes, over, and over, and
over.

Chr. *And did the Father reveal his
Son to you ?*

Hopef. Not at the first, nor second, nor third, nor fourth, nor fifth,
no, nor at the sixth time neither.

Chr. *What did you do then ?*

Hopef. What! why I could not
tell what to do.

Chr. *Had you not thoughts of leaving off praying ?*

Hopef. Yes, an hundred times, twice
told.

       Chr.

Chr. *And what did you* *then*
did not?

Hopef. I believed that it was
true which had been told me, viz.
That without the righteousness of
this Chrift, all the World could not
fave me: And therefore thought I with
my felf, if I leave off, I die; and I
can but die at the Throne of Grace.
And withall, this came into my
mind, *If it tarry, wait for it, because*
it will furely come, and will not tarry. So
I continued Praying untill the Father
fhewed me his Son.

Chr. *And how was he revealed unto*
you?

Hopef. I did *not* fee him with my
bodily eyes, but with the eyes of
mine underftanding; and thus it was.
One day I was very fad, I think fader
then at any one time in my life; and
this fadness was through a frefh fight
of the greatnefs and vilenefs of my
fins: And as I was then looking for
nothing but *Hell*, and the everlaft-
ing damnation of my Soul, fuddenly,
as I thought, I faw the Lord Jefus
look down from Heaven upon me,
and faying, *Believe on the Lord Jefus*
Chrift, and thou fhalt be faved.

But

Habb. 2. 3.

Eph. 1. 18,
19.

Acts 16, 30
31.

But I replyed, Lord, I am a great, a very great sinner; and he answered, *My grace is sufficient for thee.* Then I said, But Lord, what is believing? And then I saw from that saying, [*He that cometh to me shall never hunger, and he that believeth on me shall never thirst*] That believing and coming was all one, and that he that came, that is, run out in his heart and affections after salvation by Christ, he indeed believed in Christ. Then the water stood in mine eyes, and I asked further, But Lord, may such a great sinner as I am, be indeed accepted of thee, and be saved by thee? And I heard him say, *And him that cometh to me, I will in no wise cast out.* Then I said, But how, Lord, must I consider of thee in my coming to thee, that my faith may be placed aright upon thee? Then he said, *Christ Jesus came into the World to save sinners. He is the end of the Law for righteousness to every one that believes. He died for our sins, and rose again for our justification: He loved us, and washed us from our sins in his own blood: He is Mediator* between God and us. He *ever liveth to make intercession for us.*

2 Cor. 12. 9

Joh. 6. 35.

Joh. 6. 36.

1 Ti. 1. 15
Rom. 10. 4.
chap. 4.
Heb. 7. 24,
25

O   From

From all which I ....
must look for righte....
perfon, and for fatisfa...
fins by his blood; that wh....
in obedience to his Fathe.....
and in fubmitting to the p....
thereof, was not for himfelf, ...
him that will accept it for his fa...
tion, and be thankful. And now ...
my heart full of joy, mine eye...
of tears, and mine affections run....
over with Love to the Name, Peo....
and Ways of Jefus Chrift.

Chr. *This was a Revelation of Chr...*
your foul indeed: But tell me particula....
ly what effect this had upon your fpi....

Hopef. It made me fee that all the
World, notwithftanding all the
righteoufnefs thereof, is in a ftate
of condemnation. It made me fee
that God the Father, though he be
juft, can juftly juftifie the coming
finner: It made me greatly afhamed
of the vilenefs of my former life,
and confounded me with the fenfe of
mine own Ignorance; for there never
came thought into mine heart before
now, that fhewed me fo the beauty
of Jefus Chrift. It made me love a
holy life, and long to do fomething
for

for the Honour and Glory of the name of the Lord Jesus. Yea I thought, that had I now a thousand gallons of blood in my body, I could spill it all for the sake of the Lord Jesus.'

I then saw in my Dream, that *Hopeful* looked back and saw *Ignorance*, whom they had left behind, coming after. *Look*, said he to *Christian, how far yonder Youngster loitereth behind.*

Chr. Ay, Ay, I see him; he careth not for our Company.

Hopef. *But I tro, it wouldnot have hurt him, had he kept pace with us hitherto.*

Chr. That's true, but I warrant you he thinketh otherwise

Hope. *That I think he doth, but however let us tarry for him.* So they did.

Then *Christian* said to him, *Come away man, why do you stay so behind?*

Ignor. I take my pleasure in walking alone, even more a great deal then in Company, unless I like it the better.

Then said *Christian* to *Hopeful* (but softly) *Did I not tell you, he cared not*

Young Ignorance comes up again.

Their talk.

for

for our Company? ... _up, and let us talk away ..._ _solitary place._ Then ... Speech to _Ignorance_, he ... _how do you? how stands it betwixt ... and your Soul now?_

Ignor. I hope well, for I ... ways full of good motions, that ... into my mind to comfort me ... walk.

Chr. _What good motions? pray ... us._

Ignor. Why, I think of God and Heaven.

Chr. _So do the Devils and damned Souls._

Ignor. But I think of them, and defire them.

Chr. _So do many that are never like to come there:_ The Soul of the Sluggard defires and hath nothing.

Ignor. But I think of them, and leave all for them.

Chr. _That I doubt, for leaving ... all is an hard matter, yea a harder matter then many are aware of. But why, or by what, art thou perfwaded that thou haft left all for God and Heaven?_

Ignor. My heart tells me fo.

Chr.

Chr. *The wise man sayes,* He that trusts his own heart is a fool.

Ignor. This is spoken of an evil heart, but mine is a good one.

Chr. *But how dost thou prove that?*

Ignor. It comforts me in the hopes of Heaven.

Chr. *That may be, through its deceitfulness, for a mans heart may minister comfort to him in the hopes of that thing, for which he yet has no ground to hope.*

Ignor. But my heart and life agree together, and therefore my hope is well grounded.

Chr. *Who told thee that thy heart and life agree together?*

Ignor. My heart tells me so.

Chr. *Ask my fellow if I be a Thief: Thy heart tells thee so! Except the word of God beareth witness in this matter, other Testimony is of no value.*

Ignor. But is it not a good heart that has good thoughts? And is not that a good life that is according to Gods Commandments?

Chr. *Yes, that is a good heart that hath good thoughts; and that is a good life that is according to Gods Commandments: But it is one thing indeed to*

O 3   *have*

have forts, and think fo.

Ignor. Pray what conntry thoughts, and a life acce Gods Commandments?

Chr. There are good thoug vers kinds, fome refpecting fome God, fome Chrift, and things.

Ignor. What be good though fpecting our felves?

Chr. Such as agree with the God.

Ignor. When does our though our felves agree with the Word God?

Chr. When we pafs the fame ment upon our felves which the paffes: To explain my felf. The of God faith of perfons in a natural dition, There is none Righteou there is none that doth good.

Rom. 3.
Gen. 6. 2. *alfo,* That every imagination of heart of man is only evil, and continually. *And again,* The ima nation of mans heart is evil from Youth. *Now then, when we think of our felves, having fenfe thereof, are our thoughts good ones, becaufe cording to the Word of God.*

Ignor

Ignor. I will never believe that my heart is thus bad.

Chr. Therefore thou never hadst one good thought concerning thy self in thy life. But let me go on : As the Word passeth a Judgement upon our HEART, so it passeth a Judgement upon our WAYS; and when our thoughts of our HEARTS and WAYS agree with the Judgment which the Word giveth of both, then are both good, because agreeing thereto.

Ignor. Make out your meaning.

Chr. Why, the Word of God saith, That mans ways are crooked ways, not good, but perverse: It saith, They are naturally out of the good way, that they have not known it. Now when a man thus thinketh of his ways, I say when he doth sensibly, and with heart-humiliation thus think, then hath he good thoughts of his own ways, because his thoughts now agree with the judgment of the Word of God.

Pf. 125. 5.
Pro. 2. 15.
Rom. 3.

Ignor. What are good thoughts concerning God ?

Chr. Even (as I have said concerning our selves) when our thoughts of God do agree with what the Word saith of him. And that is, when we think of

O 4   *his*

his Being and ... hath taught: Of which ... discourse at large. But to ... with reference to us, Then we ... thoughts of God, when we think ... knows us better then we know ... and can see sin in us, when ... we can see none in our selves; ... think he knows our in-most ... and that our heart with all its ... is alwayes open unto his eyes; ... when we think that all our Righteousness stinks in his Nostrils, and ... therefore he cannot abide to see us ... before him in any confidence even in ... our best performances.

Ignor. Do you think that I am ... a fool, as to think God can see ... further then I? or that I would come ... to God in the best of my performances?

Chr. Why, how dost thou think this matter?

Ignor. Why, to be short, I think I must believe in Christ for Justification.

Chr. How! think thou must believe in Christ, when thou seest not thy need of him! Thou neither seest thy original, nor actual infirmities, but hast such opin-

opinion of thy self, and of what thou doeft, as plainly renders thee to be one that did never fee a necessity of Chrifts perfonal righteoufnefs to juftifie thee before God: How then doft thou fay, I believe in Chrift?

Ignor. I believe well enough for all that.

Chr. *How doeft thou believe?*

Ignor. I believe that Chrift died for finners, and that I fhall be juftified before God from the curfe, through his gracious acceptance of my obedience to his Law: Or thus, Chrift makes my Duties that are Religious, acceptable to his Father by vertue of his Merits; and fo fhall I be juftified.

Chr. *Let me give an anfwer to this confeffion of thy faith.*

1. Thou believeft with a Fantaftical *Faith, for this faith is no where defcribed in the Word.*

2. Thou believeft with a Falfe *Faith, becaufe it taketh Juftification from the perfonal righteoufnefs of Chrift, and applies it to thy own.*

3. This faith maketh not Chrift a Juftifier of thy perfon, but of thy actions, and of thy perfon for thy actions fake, which is falfe. 4. *There-*

... even such as will ...
in the day of God Almighty.
Justifying Faith puts the ...
sible of its lost condition by the ...
on flying for refuge unto Christ...
ousness: (Which righteousness ...
not an act of grace, by which be ...
for Justification thy obedience ...
with God, but his personal obedi...
the Law in doing and suffering ...
what that required at our hands) ...
righteousness, I say, true faith accep...
under the skirt of which, the soul ...
shrouded, and by it presented as spot...
before God, it is accepted, and acqu...
from condemnation.

Ignor. What! would you have ...
trust to what Christ in his own per...
son has done without us! This con...
ceit would loosen the reines of our lu...
and tollerate us to live as we list: For
what matter how we live, if we may
be Justified by Christs personal righ...
teousness from all, when we believe ...
it?

Chr. Ignorance *is thy name, and*
as thy name is, so art thou; even this
thy answer demonstrateth what I say.
Ignorant *thou art of what Justifying*
                                    righ...

righteousness is, and as ignorant how to
secure thy Soul through the faith of it,
from the heavy wrath of God. Yea,
thou also art ignorant of the true
effects of saving faith in this righteousness of Christ, which is, to bow
and win over the heart to God in
Christ, to love his Name, his Word,
Ways, and People; and not as thou
ignorantly imaginest.

Hop. Ask him if ever he had Christ
revealed to him from Heaven?

*Ignor. What! You are a man for re-
velations! I believe that what both you,
and all the rest of you say about that
matter, is but the fruit of distracted
braines.*

Hop. Why man! Christ is so hid
in God from the natural apprehen-
sions of all flesh, that he cannot by
any man be savingly known, unless
God the Father reveals him to them.

*Ignor. That is your faith, but not
mine; yet mine I doubt not, is as good
as yours: Though I have not in my head
so many whimzies as you.*

Chr. Give me leave to put in a
word: You ought not so slightly to
speak of this matter: for this I will
boldly affirm, (even as my good Companion

Col. 1. 5.
Eph. 1. 18,
19.

...Companion hath ... ... can know Jesus Christ ... velation of the Father ... faith too, by which the ... hold upon Christ (if it be right) ... be wrought by the exceeding ... nefs of his mighty power; the ... ing of which faith, I perceive ... Ignorance, thou art ignorant of ... wakened then, fee thine own wretch ednefs, and flie to the Lord Jefu and by his righteoufnefs, which the righteoufnefs of God, (for himfelf is God) thou fhalt be de vered from condemnation.

The talk broke up. Igno. *You go fo faft, I cannot keep pace with you; do you go on before, I muft ftay awhile behind.*

Well Ignorance, wilt thou yet foolifh be
To flight good Counfel, ten times given
* thee?*
And if thou yet refufe it, thou fhalt
* know*
Ere long the evil of thy doing fo:
Remember man in time, ftoop, do not fear;
Good Counfel taken well, faves; there-
* fore hear:*
But if thou yet fhalt flight it, thou wilt be
The lofer (Ignorance) I'le warrant thee.

Chr.

Chr. Well, come my good *Hope-ful,* I perceive that thou and I muſt walk by our ſelves again.

So I ſaw in my Dream, that they went on a pace before, and *Ignorance* he came hobling after. Then ſaid *Chriſtian* to his companion, *It pities me much for this poor man, it will cer-tainly go ill with him at laſt.*

Hope. Alas, there are abundance in our Town in his condition; whole Families, yea, whole Streets, (and that of Pilgrims too) and if there be ſo many in our parts, how many think you, muſt there be in the place where he was born?

Chr. Indeed the Word ſaith, He hath blinded their eyes, leſt they ſhould ſee, *&c. But now we are by our ſelves, what do you think of ſuch men? Have they at no time, think you, convictions of ſin, and ſo conſequently fears that their ſtate is dangerous?*

Hopef. Nay, do you anſwer that queſtion your ſelf, for you are the elder man.

Chr. Then I ſay ſometimes (as I think) they may, but they being natu-rally ignorant, underſtand not that ſuch convictions tend to their good; and there-

therefore they (as ... *felt them, and [prosume?]* ... *tinue to flatter themselves in [the?] their own hearts.*

The good use of fear *Hopef.* I do believe as you [say], fear tends much to Mens good, [&] to make them right, at their begin[ning] to go on Pilgrimage.

Job 28. 29.
Ps. 111. 10.
Pro. 17. ch.
9. 10.
Chr. Without all doubt it doth, if [it] be right: for so says the word, The fear of the Lord is the beginning of Wisdom.

Hopef. How will you describe righ[t] fear?

Right fear.
Chr. True, or right fear, is disco[?] vered by three things.

1. By its rise. It is caufed by [fa]ving convictions for sin.

2. It driveth the soul to lay fa[st] hold of Christ for Salvation.

3. It begetteth and continueth in the soul a great reverence of God, his words, and ways, keeping it tender, and making it afraid to turn from them, to the right hand, or to the left, to any thing that may dishonour God, break its peace, grieve the Spirit, or cause the Enemy to speak reproachfully.

Hopef. Well said, I believe you have said the truth. Are we now
almost

almost got paſt the Inchanted ground?

Chr. *Why, are you weary of this* *diſcourſe ?*

Hopef. No verily, but that I would know where we are.

Chr. *We have not now above two* *Miles further to go thereon. But let us* *return to our matter. Now the Igno-* *rant know not that such convictions* *that tend to put them in fear, are for* *their good, and therefore they ſeek to* *ſtifle them.*

Hopef. How do they ſeek to ſtifle them ?

Chr. 1. They think that thoſe fears are wrought by the Devil (though indeed they are wrought of God) and thinking ſo, they reſiſt them, as things that directly tend to their over-throw. 2. They alſo think that theſe fears tend to the ſpoiling of their faith, (when alas for them, poor men that they are! they have none at all) and therefore they harden their hearts againſt them. 3. They pre-ſume they ought not to fear, and therefore, in deſpite of them, wax pre-ſumptuouſly confident 4. They ſee that theſe fears tend to take away from them their pitiful old ſelf-holi-neſs,

... ... and therefore ...
with all their might.

Hope. I know something ...
my self; for before I know ...
it was so with me.

*Chr. Well, we will leave ...
time our Neighbour* Ignorance ...
*himself, and fall upon another ...
ble question.*

Talk about
one Tem-
porary.
Where he
dwelt.

Hopef. With all my heart, but ...
shall still begin.

*Chr. Well then, did you not ...
about ten years ago, one* Temporary ...
*your parts, who was a forward ...
Religion then?*

Hope. Know him! Yes, he dwelt
in *Graceless*, a Town about two miles
off of *Honesty*, and he dwelt next door
to one *Turn-back*.

*Chr. Right, he dwelt under the same
roof with him. Well, that man was
much awakened once; I believe that
then he had some sight of his sins, and
of the wages that was due thereto.*

Hope. I am of your mind, for (my
House not being above three miles
from him) he would oft times come
to me, and that with many tears.
Truly I pitied the man, and was not
altogether without hope of him;
but

but one may see it is not every one that cries, *Lord, Lord*.

Chr. *He told me at once, That he was resolved to go on Pilgrimage as we do now; but all of a sudden he grew acquainted with one* Save-self, *and then he became a stranger to me.*

Hope. Now since we are talking about him, let us a little enquire into the reason of the suddain backsliding of him and such others.

Chr. *It may be very profitable, but do you begin.*

Hope. Well then, there are in my judgement four reasons for it.

1. Though the Consciences of such men are awakened, yet their minds are not changed: therefore when the power of guilt weareth away, that which provoked them to be Religious, ceaseth. Wherefore they naturally turn to their own course again: even as we see the Dog that is sick of what he hath eaten, so long as his sickness prevails, he vomits and casts up all; not that he doth this of a free mind (if we may say a Dog has a mind) but because it troubleth his Stomach; but now when his sickness is over, and so his

P   Stomach

Stomach [...] [...]
at all alienate from [...]
turns him about and [...]
so it is true which is written [...]
is turned to his own vomit again [...]

2 Pet. 2. 22. I say being hot for Heaven, [...]
only of the sense and fear of [...]
ments of Hell, as their sense of [...]
and the fears of damnation [...]
and cools, so their desires for [...]
ven and Salvation cool also [...]
then it comes to pass, that [...]
their guilt and fear is gone, their [...]
fires for Heaven and Happiness [...]
Pro. 29,25 and they return to their course [...]

2*ly*. Another reason is, They [...]
slavish fears that do over-[...]
them. I speak now of the fears [...]
they have of men: *For the fear [...]
men bringeth a snare.* So then, though [...]
they seem to be hot for Heaven, [...]
long as the flames of Hell are ab[...]
their ears, yet when that terror [...]
a little over, they betake themsel[...]
to second thoughts; namely, [...]
'tis good to be wise, and not to r[...]
(for they know not what) the ha[...]
zard of loosing all; or at least, [...]
bringing themselves into unavoid[...]
ble and un-necessary troubles: and [...]

3ly. The shame that attends Religion, lies also as a block in their way; they are proud and haughty, and Religion in their eye is low and contemptible: Therefore when they have lost their sense of Hell and wrath to come, they return again to their former course.

4ly. Guilt, and to meditate terrour, are grievous to them, they like not to see their misery before they come into it. Though perhaps the sight of it first, if they loved that sight, might make them flie whither the righteous flie and are safe; but because they do, as I hinted before, even shun the thoughts of guilt and terrour, therefore, when once they are rid of their awakenings about the terrors and wrath of God, they harden their hearts gladly, and chuse such ways as will harden them more and more.

Chr. *You are pretty near the bufinefs, for the bottom of all is, for want of a change in their mind and will. And therefore they are but like the Fellon that ftandeth before the Judge, he quakes and trembles, and feems to re*

pent

... all is, the fear of ...
detestation of the ...
because, let but this ...
berty, and he will be a ...
a Rogue still; whereas, if ...
changed, he would be other...

Hope. Now I have ...
the reasons of their going ...
you shew me the manner ...

How the
Apostate
goes back.

Chr. So I will willingly ...

1. They draw off their ...
all that they may, from the re...
brance of God, Death, and ...
ment to come.

2. Then they cast off by ...
private Duties, as Closet-...
curbing their lusts, watching ...
row for sin, and the like.

3. Then they shun the com...
of lively and warm Christians ...

4. After that, they grow ...
publick Duty, as Hearing, Rea...
Godly Conference, and the like ...

5. Then they begin to pick ...
as we say, in the Coats of som...
the Godly, and that devilishly ...
they may have a seeming colour ...
throw Religion (for the sake of ...
infirmity they have spied in them) ...
hind their backs.   6. Th...

6. Then they begin to affociate, and affociate themfelves with carnal loofe and wanton men.

7. Then they give way to carnal and wanton difcourfes in fecret; and glad are they if they can fee fuch things in any that are counted honeft, that they may the more boldly do it through their example.

8. After this, they begin to play with little fins openly.

9. And then, being hardened, they fhew themfelves as they are. Thus being lanched again into the gulf of mifery, unlefs a Miracle of Grace prevent it, they everlaftingly perifh in their own deceivings.

Now I faw in my Dream, that by this time the Pilgrims were got over the Inchanted Ground, and entering in the Countrey of *Beulah*, whofe Air was very fweet and pleafant, the way lying directly through it, they folaced themfelves there for a feafon. Yea, here they heard continually the finging of Birds, and faw every day the flowers appear in the earth: and heard the voice of the Turtle in the Land. In this Countrey the Sun fhineth night and day; wherefore

Ifa. 6a. 4.
Cant. 2. 10,
11, 12.

P 3   this

... was ... ...
... *... of death*, ...
reach of (visible ...)
could they from this place ...
as fee *Doubting-Caſtle*. ...
were within ſight of the ...
were going to: alſo here ...
some of the Inhabitants ...
in this Land the ſhining ...
monly walked, becauſe it ...
the Borders of Heaven. In this
alſo the contract between ...
and the Bridgroom was ...
Yea here, *as the Bridegroom* ...
over the Bride, ſo did their God ...
over them. Here they had no ...
Corn and Wine; for in this place ...
met with abundance of what ...
had ſought in all their Pilgrim...
Here they heard voices from out ...
the City, loud voices; ſaying, ...
ye to the daughter of Zion, ...
thy Salvation cometh, behold ...
ward is with him. Here all the In...
bitants of the Countrey called ...
The holy People, The redeemed of ...
Lord, Sought out, &c.

Now as they walked in this Land
they had more rejoicing then ...
parts more remote from the King...
dom

Iſa. 62. 5.

ver 2.

ver. 11.

ver. 12.

Angels

dom to which they were bound; and drawing near to the City, they had yet a more perfect view thereof. It was builded of Pearls and precious Stones, also the Street thereof was paved with Gold, so that by reason of the natural glory of the City, and the reflection of the Sun-beams upon it, *Christian*, with desire fell sick, *Hopeful* also had a fit or two of the same Disease: Wherefore here they lay by it a while, crying out because of their pangs, *If you see my Beloved, tell him that I am sick of love.*

But being a little strengthened, and better able to bear their sickness, they walked on their way, and came yet nearer and nearer, where were Orchards, Vineyards and Gardens, and their Gates opened into the Highway. Now as they came up to these places, behold the Gardener stood in the way; to whom the Pilgrims said, Whose goodly Vineyards and Gardens are these? He answered, They are the Kings, and are planted here for his own delights, and also for the solace of Pilgrims. So the Gardiner had them into the Vineyards,

Deut 23. 24.

P 4 and

and bad them ... with the Damsels ... them *there* the Kings ... *Arbors* where he delight... And here they tarried and ...

Now I beheld in my ... they talked more in their ... this time, then ever they di... their Journey; and being ... there about, the Gardiner ... to me, Wherefore musest ... the matter? It is the nature ... fruit of the Grapes of thes... yards to go down so sweetly... cause the lips of them that are ... to speak.

So I saw that when they ... they addressed themselves to ... to the City. But, as I said, ...

Revel. 11. 18 flections of the Sun upon the ... (for the City was pure Gold) ... extreamly glorious, that they ... 2 Cor. 3. 18. not, as yet, with open face be... it, but through an *Instrument* ... for that purpose. So I saw, tha... they went on, there met them ... men, in Raiment that shone ... Gold, also their faces shone as ... light.

These men asked the Pilgri... whe...

whence they came? and they told them; they also asked them, Where they had lodg'd, what difficulties, and dangers, what comforts and pleasures they had met in the way? and they told them. Then said the men that met them, You have but two difficulties more to meet with, and then you are in the City.

Christian then and his Companion asked the men to go along with them, so they told them they would; but, said they, you must obtain it by your own faith. So I saw in my Dream that they went on together till they came within sight of the Gate.

Now I further saw that betwixt them and the Gate was a River, but *Death.* there was no Bridge to go over, the River was very deep; at the sight therefore of this River, the Pilgrims were much stounded, but the men that went with them, said, You must *Death is* go through, or you cannot come at *not wel-* the Gate. *come to nature,*

The Pilgrims then, began to en- *though by* quire if there was no other way to *it we pass* the Gate; to which they answered, *out of this* Yes, but there hath not any, save *World into* two, *glory.*

1 Cor 15.
51 52.

... in ...
permitted to ... ...
the foundation of ...
shall, untill the last ...
found. The Pilgrims ...
ally *Christian*, began to ... ...
mind, and looked this way ...
but no way could be found ...
by which they might ...
River. Then they ask ...
if the Waters were all of ...
They said, No; yet they ...

*Angels
help as not
comforta-
bly through
death.*

help them in that Cafe, for ... ...
*You shall find it deeper or ...
as you believe in the King of the ...*

They then addressed them ... ...
the Water; and entring, *Ch...*
began to sink, and crying out ...
good friend *Hopeful*; he said, ...
in deep Waters, the Billows go ...
my head, all his Waves go over ...
Selah.

Then said the other, Be of ...
chear, my Brother, I feel the ...
tom, and it is good. Then said *C...*

Christians
conflict at
the hour of
death.

stian, Ah my friend, the forrow ...
death have compassed me abo ...
I shall not see the Land that flo ...
with Milk and Honey. And wi ...
that, a great darkness and horro ...

fell upon *Christian*, so that he could not see before him; also here he in great measure lost his senses, so that he could neither remember nor orderly talk of any of those sweet refreshments that he had met with in the way of his Pilgrimage. But all the words that he spake, still tended to discover that he had horror of mind, and hearty fears that he should die in that River, and never obtain entrance in at the Gate: here also, as they that stood by, perceived, he was much in the troublesome thoughts of the sins that he had committed, both since and before he began to be a Pilgrim. 'Twas also observed, that he was troubled with apparitions of Hobgoblins and Evil Spirits. For ever and anon he would intimate so much by words. *Hopeful* therefore here had much adoe to keep his Brothers head above water, yea sometimes he would be quite gone down, and then ere a while he would rise up again half dead. *Hopeful* also would endeavour to comfort him, saying, Brother, I see the Gate, and men standing by it to receive us.

But

[...] Christian [...]
be you they [...]
Hopeful ever since [...]
so have you, said he to [...]
Brother, said he, surely if [...]
he would now arise to help [...]
for my sins he hath brought [...]
the snare, and hath left me [...]
said *Hopeful*, My Brother, you [...]
quite forgot the Text, where [...]

Psal. 73. 4. of the wicked, *There is no* [...]
their death, but their strength [...]
they are not troubled as other [...]
ther are they plagued like other [...]
These troubles and distresses that [...]
go through in these Waters, are [...]
sign that God hath forsaken you, [...]
are sent to try you, whether you [...]
call to mind that which hereto [...]
you have received of his good [...]
and live upon him in your distress [...]

Then I saw in my Dream, [...]
Christian was as in a muse a while [...]
To whom also *Hopeful* added [...]
word, *Be of good chear,* [...]

Christian *Christ maketh thee whole:* And [...]
delivered that, *Christian* brake out with a loud
from his voice, Oh I see him again! and [...]
tears in
death. tells me, *When thou passest through*
Isa. 43. 2. *the waters, I will be with thee,* [...]
through [...]

through the Rivers, they shall not over-flow thee. Then they both took courage, and the enemy was after that as ftill as a ftone, untill they were gone over. *Chriftian* therefore prefently found ground to ftand up-on ; and fo it followed that the reft of the River was but fhallow. Thus they got over. Now upon the bank of the River, on the other fide, they faw the two fhining men again, who there waited for them. Where-fore being come up out of the River, my faluted them faying, *We are mi-niftring Spirits , fent forth to minifter for thofe that fhall be Heirs of Salva-tion.* Thus they went along towards the Gate, now you muft note that the City ftood upon a mighty hill, but the Pilgrims went up that hill *with eafe,* becaufe they had thefe two men to lead them up by the Arms; alfo they had left their *Mortal* Gar-ments behind them in the River; for though they went in with them, they came out without them. They there-fore went up here with much agi-lity and fpeed, though the founda-tion upon which the City was fram-ed was higher then the Clouds. They

The Angels do wait for them fo foon as they are paffed out of this world.

They have put off mortality

[They ...] Regions of the [air] as they went, [being ...] cause they safely got [over] and had such glorious [...] to attend them.

The talk they had with [the Shining] Ones, was about the Glory [of the] place, who told them, that [the beauty] and glory of it was ine[xpressible.] Heb. 12. There, said they, is the Mo[unt Sion,] 22 23, 24 the Heavenly *Jerusalem*, the [innume-] Rev. 2. 7. rable Company of Angels, [and the] Rev. 3. 4. Spirits of Just men made [perfect.] You are going now, said [they,] to the Paradice of God, [wherein] you shall see the Tree of Life, [and] eat of the never-fading fruits [there-] of: And when you come there, [you] shall have white Robes given [you,] and your walk and talk shal[l be] every day with the King, eve[n all] the days of Eternity. There [you] Rev. 21. 1. shall not see again, such things [as] you saw when you were in the [lower] Region upon the Earth, to wit, so[r-] row, sickness, affliction, and dea[th,] *for the former things are passed away.* Isa. 57. 1. 2. You are going now to *Abraham, to* *Isaac,* and *Jacob*, and to the Pro[-] phets

Prophets; men that God hath taken away from the evil to come, and that are now resting upon their Beds, each one walking in his righteousness. The men then asked, What must we do in the holy place? To whom it was answered, You must there receive the comfort of all your toil, and have joy for all your sorrow; you must reap what you have sown, even the fruit of all your Prayers and Tears, and sufferings for the King by the way. In that place you must Gal. 6. 7. wear Crowns of Gold, and enjoy the perpetual sight and Visions of the Holy One, *for there you shall see him as* Joh. 3. 2. *be is.* There also you shall serve him continually with praise, with shouting and thanksgiving, whom you desired to serve in the World, though with much difficulty, because of the infirmity of your flesh. There your eyes shall be delighted with seeing, and your ears with hearing, the pleasant voice of the mighty One. There you shall enjoy your friends again, that are got thither before you; and there you shall with joy receive, even every one that follows into the Holy Place after you.

There

Jude 14.
Da.7.9,10.
1 Cor. 6.
v. 3.

with Glory ... into an equal ... the King of Glory, ... come with found of ... Clouds, as upon the ... Wind, you shall come ... when he shall sit upon the ... Judgement, you shall ... yea, and when he shall ... upon all the workers of ... them be Angels or Men ... shall have a voice in that Ju... becaufe they were his and ... nemies. Alfo when he shall return to the City, you shall ... with found of Trumpet, ... with him.

Now while they were thus ... ing towards the Gate, behold, a ... pany of the Heavenly Hoft ... out to meet them: To whom ... faid, by the other two fhining ... Thefe are the men that have ... our Lord, when they were in ... World; and that have left all ... his holy Name, and he hath fent ... to fetch them, and we have brought ... them thus far on their defired Jour... ney; that they may go in and look ...

their Redeemer in the face with joy. Then the Heavenly Host gave a great shout, saying, *Blessed are they that are called to the Marriage supper of the Lamb*: and thus they came up to the Gate.

Revel. 19.

Now when they were come up to the Gate, there was written over it, in Letters of Gold, *Blessed are they that do his commandments, that they may have right to the Tree of life; and may enter in through the Gates into the City.*

Re. 22. 14.

Then I saw in my Dream, that the shining men bid them call at the Gate, the which when they did, some from above looked over the Gate; to wit, *Enoch*, *Moses*, and *Elijah*, &c. to whom it was said, These Pilgrims, are come from the City of *Destruction*, for the love that they bear to the King of this place: and then the Pilgrims gave in unto them each man his Certificate, which they had received in the beginning; Those therefore were carried into the King, who when he had read them, said, Where are the men? To whom it was answered, They are standing without the Gate, the King then

Q   com-

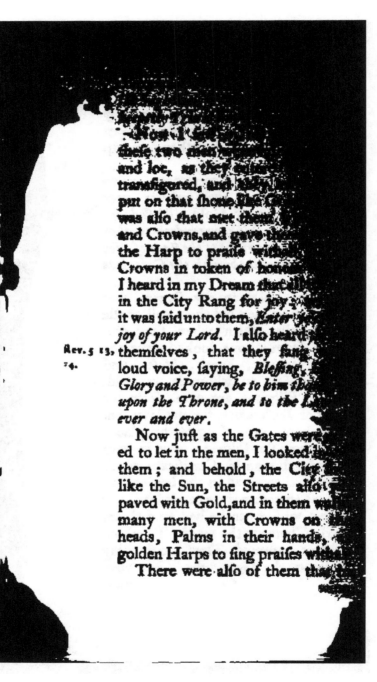

Now I [saw] ... these two men ... and lot, as they ... transfigured, and ... put on that shone. The ... was also that met them, ... and Crowns, and gave ... the Harp to praise with ... Crowns in token of honour ... I heard in my Dream that all ... in the City Rang for joy; ... it was said unto them, *Enter ... joy of your Lord.* I also heard ...

Rev. 5. 13, 74. themselves, that they sung ... loud voice, saying, *Blessing, ... Glory and Power, be to him that ... upon the Throne, and to the L[amb] ... ever and ever.*

Now just as the Gates were ... ed to let in the men, I looked in ... them; and behold, the City ... like the Sun, the Streets also ... paved with Gold, and in them w[alked] ... many men, with Crowns on ... heads, Palms in their hands, ... golden Harps to sing praises with ...

There were also of them that ...

wings, and they answered one another without intermission, saying, *Holy, Holy, Holy, is the Lord*. And after that, they shut up the Gates: which when I had seen, I wished my self among them.

Now while I was gazing upon all these things, I turned my head to look back, and saw *Ignorance* come up to the River side; but he soon got over, and that without half that difficulty which the other two men met with. For it happened that there was then in that place one *Vain-hope* a Ferry-man, that with his Boat helped him over: so he, as the other I saw, did ascend the Hill to come up to the Gate, only he came alone; neither did any man meet him with the least incouragement. When he was come up to the Gate, he looked up to the writing that was above; and then began to knock, supposing that entrance should have been quickly administred to him: But he was asked by the men that lookt over the top of theGate, Whencecame you? and what would you have? He answered, I have eat and drank in the presence of the King, and he has

Q 2

taught

... they ... ...
King. So he ...
for one, and found ...
they, Have you no ...
answered never a wor...
told the King, but ...
come down to see. ...
manded the two shini...
conducted *Christian* and ...
the City, to go out and ...
rance and bind him hand ...
and have him away. The...
him up, and carried him thro...
air to the door that I saw in the...
the Hill, and put him in there. ...
saw that there was a way to ...
ven from the Gates of Heaven ...
as from the City of *Destruc*...
I awoke, and behold it was a ...

FINIS.

The Conclusion.

NOw Reader, I have told my Dream to thee;
     See if thou canst Interpret it to me;
Or to thy self, or Neighbour: but take heed
Of mif-interpreting: for that, instead
Of doing good, will but thy self abuse:
By mif-interpreting evil infues.
    Take heed alfo, that thou be not extream,
In playing with the out-fide of my Dream:
Nor let my figure, or fimilitude,
Put thee into a laughter or a feud;
Leave this for Boys and Fools; but as for thee,
Do thou the fubftance of my matter fee.
    Put by the Curtains, look within my Vail;
Turn up my Metaphors and do not fail:
There, if thou feekeft them, fuch things to find,
As will be helpfull to an honeft mind.
    What of my drofs thou findeft there, be bold
To throw away, but yet preferve the Gold.
What if my Gold be wrapped up in Ore?
None throws away the Apple for the Core:
But if thou fhalt caft all away as vain,
I know not but 'twill make me Dream again.

THE END.